Jack & Lydia

in the

Shadow of Sabotage

Albert E. Sisson

Copyright © 2015 Second Life Publishing
All rights reserved

Cover design by Rose Sisson and Albert Sisson
Photograph: © Can Stock Photo Inc.

This book is a work of fiction. Any resemblance to businesses, open or closed, or persons, living or dead, is purely coincidental.

Introduction

Some of the characters in this novel use language that could blister the paint on a battleship. I saw no point in burdening the reader with such colorful language. I have cleaned it up, so even a Sunday school teacher can read the book. If, instead, the reader would prefer the colorful version, feel free to add the language as you read.

The story is a violent one, but I contend that it is consistent with the world in which we live. We humans, especially in the U.S., like to believe that we are civilized and basically nonviolent. Anyone who knows history, watches the news on TV or, in the old days, read a newspaper can attest to the fact that we live in a violent world. Some people like to believe in human progress. Sadly, the main progress has been in the efficiency with which we can kill and maim.

This sounds pessimistic, but there runs a streak of good in most people. There is a goodness in the world, and we can help each other. Love and friendship are our salvation.

1
The Past Year and a Half

I was sitting at the table, which serves as my desk, gazing across my office thinking. I wasn't thinking about work. I was thinking about other things. One was my office size. The size of my office bothered me in some deep psychological way. Somehow, I didn't feel as if I warranted such a large office. If it wasn't for the furniture, it would appear to be about half an acre in size. The furniture helped break up the expanse, but it was more stuff that I didn't think was justified. I had to admit though the office came in handy doing my job.

My work table is like the old, heavy wooden tables you used to see in libraries. It has one drawer for pencils and pens but no other storage space. Our offices are paperless. All paper-based information is scanned into computers and the paper crosscut shredded. All data in the computers is encrypted for security. We have no filing cabinets. If the office is paperless, I wondered why I have a drawer for pencils and pens.

My chair is a high-tech arrangement that requires training for proper use. Somewhere in a computer is the instruction book, the paper version having been shredded per standard operating procedure. In spite of the heavy technology, it is a very comfortable chair.

In front of me, across a luxurious wall-to-wall carpet, are four comfortable chairs and a sofa around a heavy wooden coffee table. It is a nice arrangement for meetings and discussions. Past that is a set of large windows that gives me a great view of West Virginia mountains.

My work table and the coffee table were ordered custom made from local hardwood by my boss, Bob McAvoy. In fact, my whole office layout was his idea. I picked out the artwork hanging on the walls. One I prize greatly. It is a painting by my friend, Frankie Randall.

The perk that I really like is a closet. I keep a couple of business outfits in there. I come to work in relaxed clothes. If a formal business meeting pops up, I simply change clothes in my private bathroom. That is a wonderful benny.

I like my office. I just think it is a bit much. My boss said that his Chief Financial Officer (CFO) and Vice President of Operations, me, needs to have an office like this to properly impress our clients. Plus, I don't need a conference room because my office is big enough for meetings.

Our clients are people who need large buildings constructed. We focus on laying the foundations for large buildings. The company was originally a mining company. We are still digging in the earth but now with a different purpose, and we aren't restricted to the hills of West Virginia.

As for being the CFO and a VP, I am completely comfortable with that. I love finances, and I am a CPA. I led the process of converting Bob's company from a paper-based finance system to a fully computerized system when I first arrived.

Bob and his wife's family own the business. That makes it nice because we have no stockholders to satisfy. We can operate as we want as long as it is legal. Bob's wife is Jane.

In addition to Bob, another key leader is Paul Jackson. Paul is our tactical planner. He plans out the complex logistics for the large construction projects. He is unflappable under pressure and is a jewel to work with. He is a part owner, and his wife is Liz.

A third key player besides me, Mike Randall, is technically not an employee. He is our security contractor and part owner. He has a tight connection with Bob and Paul. The three were in military special ops together. Bob was a captain and the leader of the team on which Paul and Mike served. They were involved in operations that involved killing to save team members' lives, which forged a tight bond. In civilian life Bob formed a special club. Each Officer-of-the-Club had to have killed someone to preserve the life of another member. Bob, Paul and Mike are Officers-of-the-Club and there were no other officers until I showed up.

Mike's wife is Frankie. Frankie is a beautiful woman, and I love her deeply. It is a platonic love and she is very special to me.

About a year and a half ago, I found Bob and Jane in a life threatening situation while riding my motorcycle in West Virginia. Two perverts were about to rape and kill both of them until I intervened. I killed one bad actor, and Bob executed the second. Mike helped to make the killings look like a murder-suicide, and we were never suspected.

The wives, Jane, Liz, and Frankie, are associate members of the Club. They vote on critical decisions and are generally considered members.

One of the things they voted on was whether to kill me or not. It was true that I saved Bob and Jane's lives, but it was also true that I had witnessed Bob execute a man. The group didn't know if I could be trusted to keep my mouth shut for the rest of my life.

It turns out that at the time, Mike wanted to kill me. I didn't know that, but I knew my life was on the line while the group decided what to do about me. I later formed the opinion that Frankie saved my life. I think she was the holdout in the voting and argued for me to live. Other club members listened, and it was decided not to kill me. Because I had killed to save Bob and Jane, I was made an Officer-of-the-Club.

Just for the record, my opinion on how she may have voted did not depend on the fact that I love her. In fact, at the time of the vote I was awestruck by her, but the love developed much later as I got to know her.

Frankie is one of the most attractive women who I have ever met. She is physically beautiful, smart and has a wonderful character. In my opinion she is a great artist. She does oil paintings of things that inspire her. She will not sell a painting, but if you are lucky, she might give you one.

The first time I met her, I was struck by her beauty. That was a dangerous thing because Mike was there. Mike is a stone cold killer, so you don't mess with his stuff.

I have no wife. In fact, I was divorced right after killing the pervert. I do not know if it was a result of the killing or not, but it didn't help. I lost my wife and access to my two children, a boy and a girl. My wife's super rich family in Ohio forced me to sign a contract requiring me to stay at least one hundred yards away from my children. The city wasn't large enough for me to do that, and I was forced to leave the city and my job. Bob and Jane promised me help if I ever needed it, so I came to West Virginia without other viable options. They set me up in an apartment in The Cabin, and when Bob learned I was a CPA, he hired me as his CFO.

The Cabin isn't a cabin. It is more like a resort. It is a huge building with apartments in it. It is a nice place in which to live but not perfect.

Originally, there were two problems. First, it was a lonely place to live if there were no guests, which was burdensome right after losing my family. Second, there was and is a woman, Lydia Harding, living there who didn't appreciate having me as a neighbor. At the time she stayed there only weekends and summers. I thought she was crazy. She was so afraid of men that she often carried a handgun. In spite of that I cooked for her as well as for myself. It is easier to cook for two than it is for one. Besides it got her to eat with me, which was a salve on my loneliness. You know you are very lonely when you prefer eating with a crazy woman rather than alone.

She allowed no one in her apartment. She even did her own plumbing and electrical repairs. Our relationship developed without either of us intentionally doing so to the point where I was invited into her apartment.

The circumstances for the invitation were a bit extreme. My son had been kidnapped and killed, and we were returning from the funeral. Lydia invited me into her home for cheese, crackers, fruit and wine. There was no cooking involved because she did not cook. The only cooked food she got was in my apartment. That was the major reason she worked to overcome her fear of me as a man so she could eat my cooking.

I was deeply touched by both her attending my son's funeral and her inviting me into her apartment. It made me wonder about our relationship. I considered it mostly based on a growing friendship, but being invited into her apartment put a crack in the foundation of that line of thinking.

She had a rule against dating, and I had no interest in female involvement so soon after my painful divorce. She was a math professor at the time, and she was interested in physics, two favorite subjects of mine. We also discovered that we both liked dancing. Through food, math and physics discussions, and dancing, we started hanging around with each other, but our outings were declared not dates. That was her rule.

Bob has a special relationship with Lydia that he has never explained to me or, I think, to anyone else. I don't believe anyone knows why, but Bob treats Lydia like a daughter. He is very protective of her. It is one of the reasons why he lets her live in The Cabin rent free.

I know about the free rent part because one of my jobs is being the manager of The Cabin. When Bob hired me as his CFO, he made it a requirement that I live in The Cabin and that I manage it. Managing it meant taking care of the grounds, the buildings and overseeing renting The Cabin to people who liked to ski in the winter, hike in the summer, admire leaf color in the fall, and watch nature bud in the spring. I have a staff to do the actual work, but I am the manager.

I have no proof, but I suspect that Bob wanted Lydia and me to strike up a friendship. If so, it was a crazy idea. It was like putting a cat and a dog in the same box.

Speaking of cats, Lydia has a cat called Cat or The Cat. He is a huge, ugly, orange beast. Lydia rescued him from the streets of Pittsburgh. Cat doesn't like people. Perhaps his street life soured him on people. His relationship with Lydia is touchy. For reasons known only to The Cat, he likes me. This is a source of considerable friction between Lydia and me. She feels that she is owed respect because she rescued him from a life style destined to lead to a short life span. If you know anything about cats, it wouldn't surprise you that he would do something like this.

I still miss my family, but I consider myself to be very fortunate to have fallen in with such a caring group of people. I doubt that I would have survived the last year and a half without their support. Even Lydia was a godsend.

The other thing on my mind is that I am mad as hell.

We are having problems that threaten the life of Bob's business. Bob is convinced that the problems stem from what he calls "the old days." That refers to a period of time after Bob, Paul, and Mike got out of the military, and they used their military training and connections to engage in high risk, illegal activities for generating cash to convert the failed family coal company into a viable construction company. Uncle Jake, who has since passed away, cooked the company books to hide the cash intake.

Bob doesn't want me to know the details of that part of the business for legal reasons. His argument is that he wants me to be uninformed so that I can never be forced to testify in court. Yeah, okay, but I have committed five murders in his presence, and I witnessed him kill a man. That alone is enough to put us in prison for the rest of our natural lives. In fact, one killing was in Texas, and that was a capital offense.

He maintains his position, and I feel insulted and mistrusted. Our whole lives and being an Officer-of-the-Club are built upon mutual trust. I feel let down in a big way. I think Mike is on my side, but I'm not positive. Paul keeps his mouth shut. His support of Bob is a silent one. He never argues or makes supporting remarks.

I feel miserable. I apparently am good enough to kill a man to save his life and Jane's life, but I am not to be trusted in a matter that is threatening to bankrupt the company. Being CFO and a VP, I think I should be fully engaged in the matter.

The problem is that someone is sabotaging a major work site in New Jersey. If the job falls behind schedule, we stand to lose close to a billion dollars worth of future business. We could not survive losing that much business.

There is a major point of contention. I have argued for more focus on the job site in New Jersey, and Bob is arguing, and winning, for a focus on searching out participants from the old days to see who is trying to even old scores. This has gotten to the point where I wonder about Bob being paranoid. In any case he is directing Mike to use his resources to investigate the past rather than the job site.

The failure of the business is a big worry, but the thing that really sticks in my craw is the apparent mistrust. That cuts me to the quick. I am about ready to call it quits. Thinking about quitting, since it was a little after five, I decided to quit for the day.

2
Danny I

Mary Hatfield, my assistant, had already left, so I locked the offices and went to the parking lot to get in my company supplied Lexus. The car is blue, my favorite color. It is loaded with features most of which are wasted on me. I am a driver, not a fiddler of doodads.

One feature that I like a lot is that the company provides all the maintenance on the car. Oil changes, tire pressure checks, tire rotation, and you-name-it are all done for me. The company even supplies the license, gas, and insurance.

The car is a nice benny. If I resign from this job, I will be losing a lot of bennies. I could survive it. When I came here, I had no bennies.

I drove out of the parking lot slowly because I was still thinking. It is a bad habit. I decided to turn it off and concentrate on driving. West Virginia mountain roads require your full attention or punish you if you daydream.

I wasn't going into mountain switchbacks, but the roads are two lanes without a shoulder. Although there aren't any switchbacks, the roads are not straight, and at this time of day when workers are going home, there is traffic.

The Gin Mill came up on my left. I thought about stopping, but I was not in the mood for socializing. I often stop there for a couple of bourbons. I pay Red, the bartender, a few extra bucks to stock Maker's Mark. It is too high end for the standard clientèle.

Maker's Mark is a quality straight bourbon made in Kentucky. By law it has to be at least fifty-one percent corn based. I love corn. The distiller claims that the local iron-free water is a key to their whisky quality. They prefer to use the "whisky" spelling to emphasize their Scottish heritage. Other Americans insist on spelling it "whiskey."

They are required by law to age their bourbon in new, charred oak barrels. This actually is a major source of the whisky flavor. For standard whisky, white oak is used. For premium whiskies, French oak is used.

The wood is charred into an alligator pattern. The charring caramelizes the sugars in the wood and adds flavor to the whisky. In a simple way of thinking about it, the liquid provides the alcohol and the charred wood provides the flavor. Without the aging in charred wood, you have white lightning A.K.A. moonshine, which is a clear liquid. The charred wood gives the whisky its caramel color.

The barrels full of whisky are put in huge warehouses for aging. It matters where the barrel is in the warehouse. The top of the warehouse is hotter than the bottom. It is the temperature differential that moves the liquid in and out of the wood. The barrels at the top age at a different rate than those at the bottom, so the barrels are moved.

Maker's Mark age their bourbon to taste rather than time, adding to its quality. This reduces the variations caused by the temperature differences, barrel rotation, and other factors in the aging process. It is very complicated. The rules have been developed over the years, and the important details are kept a secret.

After transferring the whisky to bottles, they top them off with a red wax "seal" that has been their trademark since the 1960s. This doesn't add to the quality, but it adds to its cachet.

You can make great drinks with Maker's Mark, but I often drink it over ice. You need to drink it before the ice melts because the water dilutes the whisky too much. For that reason many people drink it without ice, but I like the chill. Anyway, all of this is too refined for The Gin Mill clientèle.

The guys in The Gin Mill get rough at times, and I occasionally help Red with some of the rowdies. I bounced for cash while going to college, so I am experienced at the art of quelling barroom disturbances.

I am on the large side. I am a little over six feet six inches in my stocking feet, depending on the thickness of my socks. I like to think of my weight as about two hundred and forty-five pounds. I lift weights on a regular basis, so I carry a lot of weight in my legs, arms and shoulders. Most of the time, guys take one look at my size and retreat, but there have been times when I had to step in. I am a trained boxer and was considered for professional boxing at one time, so if the action gets too rough, I have no problem mixing it up. I try to avoid the action. It isn't consistent with my company position.

I used to like going to The Gin Mill so I wouldn't be alone at The Cabin on week nights. I didn't socialize with the clientèle much, but I liked talking with Red. He is an okay guy, and we struck up a friendship.

I drove by The Gin Mill and continued down the highway to The Cabin. I pulled into the long macadam driveway that winds through oak and hard maple trees. Being curved, it isolates The Cabin from the road.

On the way up the drive I met Danny coming out. The driveway is one lane, but wide enough to pass if we each got partly off the pavement. Danny works for Mike in the security business. He is a nice kid and what I call old school. He works hard, doesn't do drugs and is moderate in alcohol consumption. He is engaged to a lovely young lady by the name of Bonnie. The whole gang is excitedly looking forward to their wedding.

Danny worships Mike. They hang around together,

and Mike takes Danny fishing. I don't like fishing, but I let Danny use our gun range. I often shoot with Danny, and we have a great deal of fun together. He often comes over just to hang around. Sometimes I hire him for odd jobs around The Cabin. Danny isn't related to either Mike or me, but Danny likes to call us uncles.

We have a gun range for handguns, a long range for rifles and a shotgun range for both skeet and trap shooting. There isn't much interest in sporting clay, so we don't support that.

The gun range is very well done. The local police, state police, and sheriff's department come to our range for shooting, including qualifications. That doesn't cost us a lot, and it makes for good relations with the police.

I assumed that Danny was coming from the range, and when he pulled up along side to say hi, I asked him if he had hit anything.

"Sure. You always hit something. The trick is to hit what you aim at," he replied.

"So, did you hit anything you aimed at or did you hit something and then decide that was what you aimed at?"

"I did all right."

"Are you still planning on getting married?"

"Yes sir, looking forward to it."

"So am I. Well, see you later."

I drove on up the drive and The Cabin came into view.

* * *

Danny drove on down the drive. His exchange with Uncle Jack was worrisome. He seemed tense and distant. It wasn't the old Jack that Danny knew and loved. He had been this way for weeks, and it worried Danny, but there was nothing he could do about it.

3
The Cabin

As many times I have driven up to The Cabin, I am still awestruck by it size and beauty. It is a huge two story building made of local woods and a combination of split blue-stone and red-stone. It has a third floor, the basement, which is carved out of solid rock. That was expensive, but Bob's company specializes in digging foundations, so it didn't cost as much as it would have for most people.

The Cabin is located on the side of a hill, so the top floor is level with the parking lot. The front lawn is level with the first floor and slopes down to a man-made lake.

There are miles of hiking trails and several bridle paths for our guests. Lydia and I run on the hiking trails. We both like to run several miles each day in the morning. I hired a guy, Marty, to groom the trails and to keep up all of the landscape. It is a major job, so I hired a couple of assistants for Marty. Marty often is very busy with our organic farm, so I am thinking about hiring another assistant for him.

Marty and I have a side business of growing organic vegetables. We sell most of them, but I also freeze and can a lot of them for Lydia and myself. It is a major operation each time we can or freeze. At the same time we can or freeze food for Marty's family. Marty's wife, Louise, helps with the work. She also cleans The Cabin and does our laundry. All of it is a lot of work, but she has a staff to help her.

In the basement is a high security wine cellar and walk-in gun safe. We keep handguns, shotguns, rifles and ammunition in the gun safe. They are used by the members of The Club and by certain guests with special permission. The wine cellar is stocked with a large variety and quantity of wines. Only Bob and I have access to these areas.

Also in the basement is a workout area. Bob originally wanted the workout room on the first floor so people could see the scenery while working out. The architect couldn't do that with all the other requirements, so Bob had cameras installed that project the outside scene on one wall of the workout room. It is a wonderful use of modern technology.

The Cabin is built like a resort with individual apartments. Lydia has an apartment, and I have one. Bob and Jane have a large apartment although if it is busy, we sometimes rent their apartment.

On the first floor are all of the common areas and some apartments that we rent. There is a large kitchen in which a gourmet chef would be happy. Off the kitchen is a dining room. Next to the dining room is a common area that can be used for dancing or socializing. Off to the side through double doors is a library. Bob maintains a good selection of books on science, history, biographies and autobiographies. When he has time, he likes to read in the library.

There is a small wet bar in the library as well as a large wet bar in the common area. Both bars are stocked with quality liquors, which are locked. Guests are allowed to drink the liquor if they pay an extra fee.

Leading off the dining and common areas is a set of doors going to a large patio. On one end of the patio is a huge gas grill made of split blue-stone and red-stone so it blends seamlessly into the main structure. The patio floor is made of the same split stone. There are tables, chairs, and chaise lounges.

The Cabin wall by the patio is two story glass. It is on the south side of the building, so in the winter we gather heat from the sun. In the summer when there is direct sunlight, there are shades that automatically close partially or fully depending on the amount of sunlight.

There is a flat lawn area by the patio, and then the land rolls down the hill to the lake. We have a dock where we keep a couple of pontoon boats and some smaller boats. No fueled-motor boats other than the pontoon boats are allowed. We provide electric motor boats for fishing. The lake is stocked with fish for friends and guests to try to catch.

The largest apartments are on the second floor, which can be accessed from the parking lot through a common door. The common door opens to a balcony over the downstairs common area. From the balcony you can look down on the common area and also through the large glass wall out to the patio. One can go down to the first floor common area by a curved set of stairs or down the hallway to an elevator that takes you to the first floor near the kitchen. Close to this area is a large laundry room, which can be used by guests and as well as Louise. The elevator also goes to the basement.

My apartment is moderately sized. I have a nice kitchen and a dining area. Next to the dining area is the living room. I have two bedrooms, one that I use for an office and library. I have a lot of space, but still, sometimes I feel cramped because when I was married, I lived in a huge house owned by my wife's parents. We had three floors besides the basement. I had my own den on the third floor where I could read and study my physics and math books.

The thing I like the most about The Cabin is all the woodwork. The wood is of high quality and fitted to perfection. Most of it is oak, cherry and maple. It must have cost Bob a fortune.

In my early days here, the only drawback was the loneliness. However, I ensconced myself in my apartment, listened to music or read. Reading is a great getaway. You can go any place in the world or out of this world and have any kind of adventure that you like with a good book. I also enjoyed cooking.

Now the loneliness is broken by Lydia showing up to eat or talk, and she uses my office to work. Life in The Cabin isn't so bad now.

4
The Rock

I changed my clothes and headed for The Rock. I found The Rock in a nearby field. The field is sloped and covered with dry grass in the summer. Near the top of the hill is a rock that reminds me of a place where my sister and I used to play when were kids.

She died when she was a girl and The Rock brings back pleasant and, occasionally, sad memories of those days. Sometimes in the summer I can sit on The Rock and hear her laughter. I can remember sitting on the rock in our youth and watching her run through the field of grass. In August the grass would be waist high since no farmer harvested the grass. During the dry part of the season the grass would be golden in color. I can close my eyes and see her still as she ran and laughed, usually because she had played a joke on me.

It was an idyllic time, a time before heartaches. We were young kids without worries of any kind. We had great parents and lived in a modest but nice house.

The rock was surrounded by blackberry canes. During blackberry season we often returned home with stained fingers and mouths.

All of that came to an end when she got sick. There were years of doctors and treatments, but in the end she died. Part of my world died with her, and I quit going to the rock.

I pushed all of that out of my mind for years, but when I came to The Cabin, I discovered this rock, which reminded me of the rock from my childhood. Strangely, the memorics came back to me, but they were not always sad. Instead, I found them somehow comforting.

It was calming to spend time on The Rock meditating and thinking. The rock became The Rock for me, a place of thought and meditation.

Lydia sometimes comes to be with me on The Rock. I made it clear to her that I enjoyed her company there, which was a little strange because The Rock was a personal place. Lydia and I have had several intimate conversations on The Rock.

It was here when she told me the details of her high

school trauma. She told me some of it in my apartment, but it was here that she told me the whole story. She was raped on a high school date. It was her first date. She hadn't dated because she was so tall. Of course the date was special to her, and then the boy raped her. The rape and how she was treated afterwards caused her to withdraw from people, especially men. When I met her, she was practically a recluse.

I also confided some of my secrets to her. Perhaps this made us better friends even when we thought we were antagonists.

Over the last year and a half we socialized a lot, but she insisted that what we were doing was not dating. She had a real hang-up about that. Everyone has hang-ups, but she has more hang-ups than a closet. They are big hang-ups, too.

I often came to The Rock to think. I am interested in Buddhism. They teach us to let go of attachments. I have not been able to do that to any great extent. I like to think that I treat my possessions more objectively than most people, but I like my Lexus. It really isn't mine, but it feels like it. I am very conscious of living without my possessions, but I enjoy living with them at the moment. To that extent, they are attachments.

Buddhists are big on meditating. The closest I have come to that is sitting on this rock and letting the world go. It centers me.

It isn't the same as meditation, but I like sitting quietly and watching Mother Nature. If you are still and quiet long enough, animals come out and go about their business of making a living. There is nothing phony or contrived. Everything they do is for their survival and the survival of their species. It quiets my mind to watch nature at work.

I also think through problems on The Rock. That is a bad practice. One ought to keep meditation and thinking places separate.

Right now I needed to think. This business with Bob was heavy on my mind, and I had to come to some sort of conclusion in the very near future.

I sat there with the sun streaming down on me. It was quiet except for the insects. Secretly, insects rule the world. We just don't realize it. They are everywhere.

See how my mind can wander? My mind has a mind of its own.

I came to West Virginia for a temporary resuscitation and ended up staying much longer than I planned. Bob clearly has plans for me staying forever. I am his backup in his company. I am sort of a life insurance policy for his family.

I didn't stay just for a job. I stayed because it felt good to be part of a group of loyal friends. I helped them, and they helped me. We shared life threatening secrets about each other. The core of this was trust.

Trust is a big deal to me. It is the fabric of life. Without trust there was nothing of value. The bottom line is that I feel that Bob does not trust me. Without that trust our whole relationship is changed into something I don't understand or value.

Was I making too much out of trust? Maybe some people would think so, but for me I think not. So the whole thing boils down to how to repair the trust or leave.

5
Lydia

Lydia was trying to finish up a contract. She had given up teaching in Pittsburgh to consult. Jack had given her the courage to take the leap. She liked teaching except for the pressures to publish, and she didn't like the departmental politics. The politics were important for getting promoted and even keeping her job.

The other drawback was the drive to Pittsburgh. It was a long drive, and in the winter time it could be a tough drive. The drive was necessary because she needed The Cabin to recharge her batteries, and she did all of her lecture planning at The Cabin. She came to The Cabin every weekend and all summer.

She was worried about Jack. For the last few weeks he had been moody and distracted. At times he was almost irritable, which was very unusual for him. He was one of the most stable and sanguine people she had ever known.

When he first moved into The Cabin, she was

resentful. She didn't know exactly why, but it irritated her that Bob and Jane let him stay in The Cabin. She wasn't exactly nice to Jack, but he always treated her with respect.

Then Cat, who basically doesn't like people, took a liking to Jack. That galled her. She had saved Cat's life, and he showed her no gratitude. In fact, he was often nasty to her. Then Cat crawled on Jack's lap and went to sleep. After that he practically moved in with Jack. Jack put in a cat door so The Cat wouldn't scratch on his door. Cat slept on Jack's bed, so Jack got a pad for him to sleep on. Jack started by giving him water. Then he installed a food dish and a litter box. Now that she thought about it, she realized The Cat had moved.

On the positive side Jack is a great cook. Probably he should be called a chef. He loves to cook. He said it was easier to cook for two than it was for one, so he invited her to eat with him. She wouldn't have done it, but she didn't know how to cook.

Until she met Jack she had no interest in cooking or in food. He opened up a whole new world for her. He cooked foods that she had never heard of, and they were delicious. He even started a truck garden business with Marty so he could grow his own organic vegetables. A year later he and Marty put in an herb garden. It was a lot of work growing your own food, but Jack had the money to hire people. She doubted if he made any money on the vegetables after expenses and hiring people, but he had great food as a result.

At first it was painful for her to go into his apartment. She had a deep fear of men. The lure of food won, but she carried her .32 caliber Kel-Tec handgun when she went into his apartment. His treatment of her was friendly and even keeled. He never once made her feel uncomfortable. After a while she felt bad about carrying and left the handgun in her apartment.

She had a rule against dating men. She went with him to a business dinner as a favor to Bob, but she refused to call it a date. Jack taught her how to dance, and they practiced before the dinner. It turned out that she had a great time and felt comfortable with Jack. It was a strange new feeling.

Jack planned the business dinner and activities. One thing he did that impressed her greatly was that he bought corsages for the women. He apparently had a liking for flowers. He also talked her into going into the woods looking for wild flowers in the spring. She didn't want to go at first. She was suspicious of his motives, but it turned out that all he wanted was company while looking for the flowers. It was a side to a man that she had never seen before. Jack was an unusual man.

They often went dancing at The Gin Mill. She liked that. One thing that made it pleasant was that no man in the place made any kind of move toward her because of Jack's size. He was a giant of a man. His size kind of put her off when she first met him, but after being around him she began to appreciate both him and his size.

For one thing it was nice to have a man taller than she. Lydia was about six feet tall. With heels she was usually taller than any man around. With Jack that was not a problem.

As she got to know Jack, she realized what a complex man he was. On the one hand he liked flowers, but on the other hand she was sure he had killed several men. She was pretty sure that he killed at least one of the perverts attacking Bob and Jane. She also was sure he killed all of the men who kidnapped and killed his son. She could understand those killings, but it seemed incongruous with the Jack she knew in The Cabin.

Jack hung around with Mike who was the security contractor for Bob's company. Mike liked Jack and came to The Cabin often to see him. They rode motorcycles together, and sometimes Bob and Paul joined them. She didn't like Mike as much. He scared her. She thought Mike was a killer. Jack seemed to like Mike, and they got along well together. It was another mystery about Jack.

The biggest mystery though was how comfortable she had gotten around him. As a result, she was more comfortable with other men and had begun to socialize. That was a huge change because she was basically a recluse before she met Jack. He somehow had a healing effect on her. She didn't know if it was a deliberate act on Jack's part or just a result of how he was. In any case, since being around Jack, she had become more like a real person.

Now Jack was not the same guy he had been. She noticed that in the last few weeks he had changed. Something was bothering him, and she decided to talk with him about it. She saw him leave The Cabin and go down a trail. She knew he was headed to his rock. She started down the same trail.

6
Two on The Rock

I wasn't getting anywhere with my thinking. My mind was going in circles. It seemed like logic would dictate my resigning. On the other hand, Bob had given me a new life when I desperately needed one. It was hard to resign from that. Back and forth, round and round my mind went with no resolution. It was making me so irritable that I couldn't stand myself.

My eye caught a movement. Lydia was coming up the trail to the field. I watched her make her way up the hill through the grass. Her long legs quickly carried her to The Rock.

She climbed up on The Rock by my side and sat down. She threaded her arm under my arm and hugged my bicep. It was something she did when she was under stress or wanted comfort from me. I sometimes thought that maybe she did it to comfort me like she did at my son's funeral.

We sat there for some time with neither of us

speaking. Finally, she started.

"Jack, what is wrong?"

"What makes you think something is wrong?"

That was the wrong thing to say. Lydia is extremely smart, and she hates it when people treat her like a dummy. I immediately regretted my question. She didn't say anything, so I started over.

"I have been thinking about resigning from Bob's company." I felt her stiffen and her fingers bit into my bicep.

She said, "You can't be serious. Bob depends on you. He has you set up to replace him in the event he is incapacitated in some way. He is counting on your leading the company and saving the business for his family. How can you even think such thoughts?"

"Well, he isn't treating me like he trusts me. Several times now he has embarrassed me in front of others by asking me to leave his office so he, Paul and Mike could talk about how to save the company from this huge crisis the business is in. Trust is important to me. You either trust me, or you don't."

"I know he trusts you. You must believe that," Lydia replied emphatically.

I continued, "He argues that he is trying to legally protect me by making it so I can deny knowledge of certain events in the past. I don't buy it. He and I have done things in front of each other that could send us to prison for the rest of our lives. How can my knowledge of what he, Paul, and Mike did years ago to generate cash be worse than that?

"Lydia, do you remember what you told me in a similar conversation about a year ago? I told you that I would never lie to you, and you claimed I was lying to you by omission. You further said that if I did tell you about some of the things I had done, you would lie in court and never give me up. I think the same line of thought applies to Bob, but he doesn't. I am fed up with the situation. Furthermore, I am sure he is wrong about the cause of the sabotaging. I don't think it is related to the old days. I think it is something else, and it is about to kill the business."

"Jack, have you confronted Bob with these

thoughts?"

"Of course, but he won't listen to me. He is too busy conjuring up paranoid theories of yesteryear. He is forcing me into a position where I think I have to resign."

"Please, you must think about this carefully," Lydia pleaded.

"What do you think I have been doing for past month or two?"

"I'm sorry. It is just that we need a little time. I put some stew in the slow cooker before I left The Cabin. It should be ready. Let's go eat."

I wondered about the "we" part of her statement. As far as I knew this was my decision and mine alone.

7
Mike Shows Up

We ate dinner together quietly. The stew was some that we had frozen. We had rolls that I baked the day before. After dinner I cleaned up the table and put the dishes in the dishwasher since Lydia had prepared dinner.

She disappeared while I was cleaning up. She usually tells me where she is going, but she didn't say a word, just disappeared.

Cat was looking at me with a disagreeable look on his face. When he saw me look at him, he put on a smile and rubbed my leg. That was a sure sign he wanted something. I looked at his food dish, and it was mostly empty. I got out the cat food and gave him his dinner. I also cleaned out his water dish and filled it with fresh water. He used to be a street cat, but now he is fussy with his water. He wants it fresh.

I had given his fresh water fetish a lot of thought. I figured that maybe the water picked up an odor or taste from the plastic, so I switched to glass. I think it might have helped a little, but it was hard to tell. I concluded that a bigger factor was that he liked to see me pour his water. Every time I gave him water, he got very excited. In fact, he got so excited that if I wasn't careful, he would step in his water dish and tip it over while I was filling it. It seemed to be very important to him, so I ended up giving him fresh water twice a day.

It is hard for me to fathom a life where a fresh bowl of water is a high point of your day. That is a great life as long as you have someone willing to give you a fresh bowl of water. Imagine being happy by getting fresh water, food, a place to sleep and the occasional petting. That is a very cool life. People are seldom satisfied. They always want more. I think we can take a lesson from The Cat.

I heard a security beep signaling that a car was coming in. I glanced at a display and saw that it was Mike's car, and probably he was driving. He has a key for the outer door. Actually, since he is the security guy, he probably has keys for everything in The Cabin except the wine cellar and the gun safe. He buzzed my apartment door.

I opened the door, and Mike came in. He looked like there was something on his mind. It was subtle. He isn't the kind of guy who lets you know much about his thinking.

He nervously looked around for The Cat who has bitten him a couple of times. Mike did something or didn't do something that displeased The Cat. I never figured out what it was, and Mike didn't seem to know. I didn't know for sure, but I imagined that Mike would like to kill The Cat for biting him. He wouldn't kill The Cat because he knew that Lydia and I liked The Cat. Life often has its frustrations.

Mike came in and sat down. I got out a couple of brandy glasses and poured two drinks of Bob's apple brandy. Mike looked tense, so I made it a double. Besides, I wanted a double. Bob made a barrel of it every year. It is excellent, and I knew Mike liked it.

I sat down and Mike started talking.

"Jack, I know things have been difficult for you at work lately. Bob hasn't been treating you right. Is there anything that I can do to help?"

"Yes, you can get him to drop this nonsense about the sabotage being the result of the old days. We need to focus our resources in New Jersey instead of tracking down these characters from the past."

Mike about made me fall out of my chair when he said, "I agree with you. I have been thinking about talking with Bob in private. I think focusing on the job site and at least stopping the sabotaging would be a good idea."

"Where is Paul on all of this?"

"He agrees with you and me, but he won't go against the Captain. With Paul, the Captain will always be the Captain."

"Well, he will be a captain without a ship if we don't get things straightened out soon."

"Jack, I came over to make a deal with you. Danny and Bonnie are getting married in a few days. Right after that they are going on a honeymoon for ten days or maybe two weeks. I propose that we see them get married, and then you and I go on a motorcycle trip for ten days to two weeks. We can use that time to relax and think things over. We can figure out what to do."

I was surprised. I had no clue this was coming. I was also suspicious. Tonight was the first time I had told anyone how troubled I was and that I was thinking of resigning. Two hours later Mike shows up with this proposal. I suspected that Lydia had phoned Frankie and told her how I felt. Frankie then told Mike to get over here and fix it.

I thought it over, and it seemed like a good plan to me. I hadn't been on a good, long ride in a long time. I didn't particularly want to think about the situation any more, but it could be an opportunity to talk with Mike and get on the same page for taking action. That could make it all worthwhile. Plus, I had a ride destination in mind.

I decided to test the waters and asked, "Who picks the trip destination?"

"You do."

"I would like to ride the Blue Ridge Parkway from end to end."

"That's great. I haven't ridden it, and it sounds like a good ride."

"The only thing is it will be a tame ride. The speed limit on the Parkway is forty-five miles per hour. There are some fun roads before and after the Parkway though."

"That's fine. We don't always have to be burning up the road."

We talked a little and made tentative plans. It was going to be a busy few days getting Danny married and getting ready for the ride. Mike went home.

Both of us would need to get new tires on our bikes, change the oil, and do a general check up. That wasn't complicated, but it would require time to get it all done.

Getting Danny married was complicated by the fact that I agreed to let them use The Cabin for the reception. They were going to be married in a church. They could have a reception there, but that would mean no booze. Danny and Bonnie wanted booze so with Bob's blessing I agreed to let them use The Cabin. We had some guests in The Cabin. I talked with them, and they had no problem with us having the reception there. In fact, I think they liked the idea because I invited them to attend.

Booze was problematical though. Some of the young hillbillies could get rowdy, so I stipulated limited wine with dinner and one free drink after dinner. After that they paid for drinks with a limited number of tickets. Then I figured that the guys would have their non-drinking friends save their tickets for them, so I was going to have tickets printed up with their names on them. The bartender wouldn't know all the guests, but if a big, hairy guy came up to the bar with Shirley's ticket, he wouldn't get a drink. And yes, Shirley could get the drink and give it to the big, hairy guy but then no more tickets. See how complex life can be?

I left the decorations, cake, favors and all the other items to the women. Frankie, Liz, Lydia and Jane seemed to thrive on that part along with Bonnie. It was going to be a big affair and expensive, so Lydia and I gave it to them for a wedding gift.

8
The Wedding

Danny and Bonnie's big day finally came. They had a nice, simple, traditional church wedding. The weather was perfect and many pictures were taken in front of the church.

The church is a Protestant one as are most churches in the hills. It is built of wood with a fifty-foot steeple. The steeple has a lightning rod on top because it gets struck by lightning occasionally. I don't know if that is a comment on the religion or not. The outside is painted white and kept in good condition with volunteer labor. There are beautiful stained glass windows in both side walls. The formal entrance is a double door painted green in front with single, plain glass windows on either side. Often people enter the church in a small side door, especially in the winter when it is cold. Today, however, the front doors were wide open, welcoming the wedding party and the guests.

Lydia sat next to me and hung on to my arm. She had

a looser grip, indicating a more relaxed mood. She was beaming and obviously happy. I guess women tend to be like that at weddings. Some cried, but I think they were happy doing so.

The bride wore white and Danny and his support group wore tuxedos. The bride's attendees wore nice handmade gowns. It made the dresses tailor-made items, better than anything you can buy.

Danny was a well-built young man just entering the prime of his life. He had shed his adolescence and was ready for adulthood. My only relationship with him was one of friendship, but still, I was proud of him. It was nice seeing young people like him coming up to take over as the older generations faded away. It helped give you confidence in the future. I was also happy for him and sincerely hoped that he and Bonnie would have a long, happy life together. She couldn't have made a better choice in a man.

Bonnie was gorgeous and radiant. It was a happy moment in her life. Her dress was beautiful as were the flowers she carried.

I sneaked a peek at Lydia. She had a smile on her face, but also another look that I had not seen before. It was if she was far away, thinking about something. I was curious as to the nature of her thoughts, but it wasn't the time or place to ask. Probably it would never be well to ask. I slipped my hand over to hold her hand. She squeezed my hand.

No wedding is complete without many photographs. I am not much for them, but I can see the value. I think women place the greater value on the photographs and use them to relive the wedding.

After the photographic session everyone moved to The Cabin where the festivities would take place. All the women had pitched in and decorated The Cabin and the patio. I hired a local band, which is pretty much unheard of today. Most people have CD music, but I wanted the kids to have a real band. I had money to burn, but I didn't want to burn it. It felt better doing nice things for my friends. Besides I looked forward to dancing with Lydia in front of a live band.

It was a great party, and I was able to keep the

drinking under control. In the middle of the fun Danny and Bonnie disappeared. They were on their way to a secret honeymoon trip.

Mike and I had spent some of the reception off to the side talking about our trip. We were psyched and ready to go.

9
Vito Bagotti

When I told Bob I wanted to take a couple of weeks off for a trip, he informed me that we were having a business dinner right after Danny's wedding. I needed to manage the dinner as usual. I could leave right after.

Vito Bagotti would be here with his wife for one day and night. I had to arrange entertainment for the afternoon and set up the formal dinner in the evening. We could have dancing after the dinner, if I wanted. Bob didn't care. What he did care about was that the day, including the dinner, must be flawless. Bagotti was in a position to influence a decision to send about a billion dollars of business to us if our current project in New Jersey was on schedule. So far that part didn't look so good hence the pressure. It was a big deal. I had arranged many dinners, so it was routine for me.

I booked Momma to serve the meals. She owns a restaurant in town. She serves good country cooking. Her daughter works for her in the restaurant. Bob has a special private room in the back of her restaurant, which he uses for business lunches and dinners.

For dinner we selected chicken marsala, roasted red potatoes and lightly sautéed uncut green beans. I supplied the potatoes, beans and greens for a salad from the organic truck garden that Marty and I owned. I felt in the mood to make a salad dressing, so we planned on that. I wanted the potatoes fully cooked but firm and the beans firm, not soggy or limp. We had worked together before, so Momma knew how to respond. I agreed to do the dessert and since cherries were in season, I planned to do cherries jubilee.

Bagotti likes guns, so we would take him to the gun range. His wife doesn't like guns, so I would have Jane, Frankie, Liz and Lydia take her to a quilt show. Some of the local ladies made amazing quilts.

There wouldn't be any drinking before or during the gun activities. After, there would be plenty of drinking. Alcohol is the oil for business deals.

As for the evening, I would provide quiet, soothing CD music and Bob's apple brandy. People could dance if they wanted. I knew Lydia and I would dance. I looked forward to it. I anticipated a smooth day and hoped it would help cement our business relationship.

Bagotti showed up with his wife. She seemed like a nice lady. I had reservations about Bagotti. I tried to keep an open mind, but there was something about the guy I didn't like.

The dinner and evening went well. We talked and danced after dinner. Lydia was with me as usual, and we danced a lot. Everyone seemed to have a good time. Bob and Bagotti talked business on the side.

The next day they left. The rest of us were still in The Cabin, and we had a meeting to assess how it went. As usual Frankie gave us her right-brain assessment. She said Bagotti was a sleaze bag. I wasn't sure how that related to business, but it correlated with my feelings. Lydia was silent. Everyone else thought we could do business with Bagotti, but that we should be careful about trusting him.

That night Lydia came to my apartment. She was nervous and hung around for a while. Finally, she said,

"Bagotti made an indecent proposal to me."

I wasn't sure I heard her right, so I had her repeat it.

"For heavens sake why didn't you speak up? If you had told me when he did it, he might not have been able to walk out of here."

"I know. That's why I didn't say anything. This business deal is very important to Bob."

"Yeah, but you are not a prostitute. You don't have to put up with this. Bob would be just as upset as I am over it."

"I know that, too. That is why I don't want you to tell him. The only reason I told you is that I want you to be aware of what kind of man he is."

"Does Frankie know about this?"

"She knows something happened, but she doesn't know the details. You are the only one who knows the details."

I was sick at heart. How was I to deal with a guy like this? I would have to keep an eye on Bagotti.

10

The Motorcycle Trip

Mike and I had gotten new tires and rode them a hundred miles or so to seat them and make sure they didn't leak or have other problems. We had bags packed, and our bikes were loaded.

Packing for a long distance motorcycle trip is a science. Only hard cased luggage on a motorcycle is waterproof. All soft luggage leaks in the rain. Mike and I both had soft luggage, so we had to put all of our stuff in sealed plastic bags. You have to squeeze all the air out before sealing the bag. Not much room in motorcycle saddlebags. A wonderful side benefit of this is that it keeps your stuff organized. I used the technique in my suitcase on business travels.

When thinking about rain on a motorcycle, most people think about umbrellas and raincoats. That works only if you are parked. On the road the water is coming at you at road speed. Think of leaving your house window open in a rainstorm. If there is no wind, not much water will get in the house. However, if there is a seventy-mile-an-hour wind blowing the rain, a lot of water is going to get in your house.

We were set. We left early in the morning and wore heavy shirts for warmth and leather jackets for protection.

I planned the trip. We were riding southwest out of West Virginia into Kentucky and then straight south until it was time to cross the mountains into Virginia. For those of you thinking that it is straighter just to go south from West Virginia to Virginia, I can only say that motorcyclist take the most fun roads, not the straight or direct ones.

We were riding through beautiful country on a two-lane blacktop road in Kentucky when a car going up the side of ridge on our left caught my eye. I wondered why a hillbilly was driving his car up through a field of tall grass. You often see strange things out in the wilds of back country. We continued a short distance and swung a hard left. I then realized we were following the hillbilly up the ridge. So who is the crazy hillbilly now?

It was a gentle slope at first, but it rapidly steepened. Then it got seriously steep and made a sharp right turn. It was such a sharp switchback that I could see marks in the pavement where cars had bottomed out on the inside of the turn. I started to sweat. I downshifted so I would have plenty of torque and not stall the motor on the turn. I scanned for traffic and fortunately there were no other mountain drivers on the road. I swung my bike to the outside of the curve and leaned into the turn, rolling on the throttle. The bike powered through, and I was on the next leg up the ridge. The road weaved through rocks too big to move, and soon we were on the ridge riding south. I still break into sweat thinking about that turn.

After a few miles we swung east and then south into Virginia and rode through hilly farm land. It continued like that until we got to the Skyline Drive.

The Skyline Drive is one hundred and five miles long. The speed limit is thirty-five, so it is not an adrenalin run. We decided to take most of the day to ride the whole length. It would be an easy, relaxing ride. After a night's rest we would start on the real attraction on our trip: The Blue Ridge Parkway.

We hit the Parkway early in the morning. The first stop was the farm at Humpback Rock. At first blush there is something romantic about the farm, but if you really look, it was a tough life living on those farms. The small house had a fireplace for heat and some light in the windowless cabin. A hinged door on the second floor let in the only light in the attic and also the cold. It must have been miserable in the winter. If it is the only thing you know, it probably is just a way of life, but it wasn't romantic. It was hard work and tough times.

Everything on the farm was either animal or human powered. All the food was obtained by hard physical labor. I had a taste of it on the truck farm Marty and I ran. However, we had machines to help us.

It was interesting to compare this cabin with The Cabin. To wash the dishes they had to lug water from a hand dug well or spring and heat it in the fireplace with hand cut wood. The bucket for lugging the water would have been a handmade wooden one. For soap they had homemade lye soap. I on the other hand dropped the dishes into a machine that washed them for me. It was mind boggling to me, but not to Mike. He was not as interested as I, and we got back on the Parkway.

The next big stop for me was Mabry Mill. This is a park now, but they have a working water-powered mill. It fascinates me to see water drop a few feet, turn a wheel and saw lumber. It is sort of like getting something for free, but of course it isn't free. There is a big investment in the race, the building, the water wheel and other machinery to make it run. I don't know why it fascinates me so. Using a natural resource to do work is not new. We do it every day. In fact, we had just burned gasoline in our bikes to create heat, which expanded gases that drove the pistons and turned the wheels. So why is the water-powered mill so mesmerizing? I think it is the simplicity. There are no chemical equations and no refineries. Most of it can be built by hand labor. For us to burn gasoline in our bikes, we had to depend on a whole industry to provide it. This mill could be built by a neighborhood of people. The saw blade and a few iron fittings had to be purchased, but most of the mill was hand built on site and ran with on-site resources. It was pretty cool. Mike let me stay there a couple of hours.

The ride was awesome. The best part of the Parkway is the southern portion in North Carolina. The mountains in North Carolina have the best motorcycling roads in the U.S. The Parkway runs right through the best of these mountains. The road runs along the top of a ridge with many pull-offs to view the spectacular scenery. The Parkway is four hundred sixty-nine miles long. It was built to connect the Shenandoah National Park with the Great Smoky Mountains National Park during the Great Depression, creating many jobs. Machinery in those days was more modest than the huge earth movers we have today. A lot of the work was done by animal and human power.

The road itself is a motorcyclist dream. The only two things keeping it from being perfect is the forty-five miles per hour speed limit and cars poking along with the occupants looking at the scenery. You are supposed to pull off the pavement to gawk, but some people cannot read, so they don't know the rules.

We finally made it to Asheville, North Carolina. I insisted that we stay in Asheville for several days to rest and to see Biltmore and a small chapel out in the country near Asheville.

Biltmore is the largest home in the U.S. at 178,926 square feet. Only 135,280 square feet is usable for living space. Bummer. I wondered about living in such a house. You could have people living in there for years and not meet them. The Cabin was big but paled in comparison to this gigantic house.

Biltmore had a lot of gardens, something The Cabin did not have except for the herb garden. Maybe we should add some. I made a note.

The chapel was a comparatively small affair, but had more meaning for me. I ran across it on a motorcycle trip with some bikers years ago when riding in the area. I was in Asheville filling my bike's gas tank along side a UPS man gassing his truck. I chatted with him. He wanted to know what we bikers were up to. I told him we were sight seeing. He said that we needed to see this little chapel out in the country in Trust, North Carolina.

He told me the story behind the chapel.

A local woman was diagnosed with cancer. She made a deal with God that if her cancer was cured, she would build a chapel. Her cancer was cured, and she built the chapel. It was small but well built of wood on a solid stone foundation. The workmanship was of high quality. It had a few pews in which visitors could sit, pray and think. It was a lovely, quiet place next to a mountain stream.

On the first visit we saw the woman in a nearby building in a kitchen. She asked us how to convert some recipe units. We asked about the background of the chapel and learned more of her story. When asked if we could donate money, we were told no. She had made a deal with God and a deal was a deal. She had to furnish the chapel, and it had to be open for all travelers.

Mike and I visited the chapel on a sunny day. We pulled our bikes off the road and went in the chapel. It was quiet inside. Mike and I spent some time there. When we came out, a guy came across the creek to talk with us. He was the current owner and was checking to see what we were up to. Not everyone had the same respect for the place that Mike and I did, and there had been some damage. Very sad to hear. He told us the woman who had built the chapel had died. It is a pretty good rule that if you find a really neat place, you should keep it as a memory and never go back. Buddha said that you can't put your foot into the same river twice. I would add that visiting the river a second time can destroy memories.

We returned to Asheville, ate dinner and went to the motel. Shortly after getting back to the motel, my cell phone rang. It was Lydia. She was crying so hard I couldn't understand what she was saying. I got her calmed down enough so she could tell me that Bob McAvoy had been shot. It felt like a body blow.

I asked if he was still alive. She thought so but wasn't sure. I asked if she was alone or if someone was with her. I was concerned because I knew how much Bob meant to her. She said Frankie was on the way over, and they were going to the hospital. She would keep me informed.

My mind was in a whirl. Maybe Bob had been right. Maybe someone from the old days was trying to even the score. For the time being I needed to get organized. First, I needed to tell Mike what was going on. We would have to cancel the rest of our trip and get back to West Virginia as soon as possible. Among other things I was now probably the acting CEO of Bob's company, and I needed to assure our clients that the business would not be affected by the shooting.

I went next door and knocked. Mike came to the door with his cell phone stuck to his ear. He motioned me into his room and in a few minutes wrapped up the call. I could see by the look on his face that he knew. He had probably just been told on the phone.

"Mike, have you heard? Bob has been shot."

"Yeah, I just talked with Frankie and Paul. Frankie is picking up Lydia and going to the hospital. Paul is at the hospital making sure Bob has the best doctors available. Liz is with Jane. Right now Paul is also acting as the security guard. He has some sheriff deputies on the way, and I am going to get my people on this right away. The first thing we have to do is make sure whoever did the shooting doesn't make another attempt on Bob's life in the hospital."

I agreed to make arrangements to get us back home as quickly as possible, which meant flying, and to make arrangements to have our bikes picked up. Mike would phone his guys to arrange security at the hospital and to start the investigation find the shooter.

I phoned Paul. I didn't want to bother him, but he needed to know what I was doing. Paul was calm as usual. He is an amazing guy. Nothing seems to shake him up. He said they didn't know if Bob was going to live or not. He was in surgery with the main surgeon and Bob's personal doctor. They were still working on him, so he was still alive.

I phoned the company pilot and gave him instructions to fly the company plane to Asheville immediately. I phoned Marty and told him to get another guy and drive my pickup truck with the motorcycle trailer to Asheville to pick up our bikes.

I found the motel manager and told him what was

going on. We needed a place to store our bikes until Marty could pick them up. The manager offered his garage at home. Turns out he was a rider.

Everything was set. I went back to my motel room. I felt antsy. There was nothing to do except wait and think. I started planning my moves as acting CEO. Maintaining clientèle confidence was a high priority. Finding the shooter was another high priority. The next few days were going to be sleepless.

11
The Wait

The flight back was smooth. Mike was as upset as I have ever seen him. He was in control, but his eyes were blacker than normal. They looked like black, shiny coals. Whether Bob lived or died, the shooter had made a big mistake. He was going to die. Mike would see to that if it took the rest of his life and all of his fortune. Of course to do so, he needed to identify the shooter. He already had his men working on it.

I was more measured. I agreed we had to find the shooter, but we also had to save the business. That was my job. I made plans as we flew. I couldn't take action until business hours, and I wanted to know if Bob was going to live before I called our clients. I also needed to talk with Jane to make sure she was okay with me acting as CEO. It was Bob's plan that I take over in a situation like this. Plans are one thing, but this was reality. She or the board might be having second thoughts as reality hit.

We landed and Paul had a car waiting to take us to

the hospital. My stomach felt like it was full of butterflies as we rushed to the waiting room. I didn't know what to expect.

When I came into the room, Lydia ran to me and gave me a huge and started crying. She was unstrung. I comforted her the best that I could. Jane's face was pale and drawn. She was calm, but the strain was obvious. Frankie was calm and keeping close to Lydia. I gave both Frankie and Liz hugs.

Paul was the strong one. He was holding things together. It was quite warm, and he had on a jacket. That told me he was carrying. I saw several other men with jackets, so they were armed. If you looked carefully, the place was crawling with armed men and as it turned out a few armed women. I didn't know how long we could keep up that level of security, but at the moment no one unauthorized was going to get close to Bob.

I hugged Jane and talked to her so no one else could hear. I asked her if it was still the board's intention that I act as the CEO until Bob recovered. She said yes. I asked if she had discussed it with the board. She said no, but that she spoke for the board. I was to take over the company until Bob was able to resume his duties. I felt like I was intruding on a family, but I told her I was ready and would start things going in the morning.

Meanwhile there was nothing much to do. I wanted a cup of coffee. Paul said he had arranged to have access to the doctor's lounge where he had placed a bag of ground gourmet coffee. He had also bought ceramic coffee cups. I hate Styrofoam cups. He was our logistics guy, and he thought of everything. I went in the lounge. Next to the coffee was a pile of Bavarian cream donuts, my favorite. Paul is a good guy.

It was like being in the army. It was hurry up and wait and wait and wait. I wanted to pace the room, but I cannot pace unnoticed. Due to my size, my pacing would make others anxious. I forced myself to sit. I sat next to Lydia, and she slid her arm under my arm and hung on tightly.

We hadn't heard a word on Bob's condition. He had been in surgery for close to six hours. The good news was that they were still working on him, and he wasn't dead. The bad news was that is a long time to be in surgery.

Time dragged. No word.

Finally, the surgeon came out and asked for Mrs. McAvoy. Jane identified herself. The surgeon told Jane Bob's condition loud enough for all of us to hear. He said that he thought Bob would live although the next twenty-four hours would be critical. Furthermore, if Bob lived, he would fully recover, but he might need physical therapy. There was plenty of time to talk about that later. He said that Bob was still in the operating room, and his personal doctor was doing the final closing, making sure that the scarring was minimized. That was Paul's doing.

We all decided to stay until Bob was in recovery. Jane would want to be there when Bob woke up, and we wanted to support Jane. Plus, I wanted to be there because surgery isn't over until the patient is awake again.

After what seemed like hours, Bob's personal doctor came into the waiting room. He said Bob was being taken to a recovery room, and a nurse would let Jane know when she could come in. The doctor was upbeat and optimistic about Bob's recovery. It could be an act. I couldn't tell.

Shortly, a nurse came in and said Jane could come into the recovery room. Jane motioned me to come with her. I didn't think that appropriate, but I followed her. Bob was groggy, but he recognized both of us. Not only was he groggy, he was goofy, too. I knew he wouldn't remember much of what was said. Jane wanted him to know that I was there, and that I had things under control. If only that were true.

As soon as it was decent to do so, I had Frankie take Lydia and me back to The Cabin. I wanted to shower, shave, have breakfast and get to the office. I wanted to update the office staff. We were a close group and people would be worried. Next, I needed to phone clients and tell them the news. I wanted to have it come from me before it hit the news media and with the Internet that wouldn't be long. I also needed to talk with Mike.

12

Where Am I? What Happened?

Bob was awake. Sort of. He could see bright lights, and he was in a bed. He wondered, why? He heard someone calling his name. He recognized the voice. It was Jane. She wanted to know if he was awake.

Bob tried to turn his head so he could see her, but his head wouldn't turn. Jesus, was he paralyzed? No, that wasn't it. He could feel resistance to his efforts to turn his head. His head was being held in place. He felt like a mummy wrapped in cloth. He couldn't move.

He wanted to speak, but he couldn't. His mouth was dry, and his throat was sore. He struggled.

Jane called for a nurse. The nurse must have been nearby or maybe even in the room because she was at his bedside almost instantly. She asked how he was doing. He tried to croak an answer. The nurse immediately recognized the problem and gave Bob a drink through a straw. It was ice water, and it was one of the best drinks he ever had. The water soothed his throat and he could speak a little.

He asked the nurse if he could have orange juice. She was looking down at him, and he could see her smile. She said she would have some sent up right away.

Jane came over to the bed and looked down at Bob. She looked like she had been up all night. Bob wondered what time it was. She told him it was early morning.

Bob was still confused. He assumed he was in a hospital because he had seen the nurse, but why was he in a hospital?

Jane said he had been shot. Shot? Why would someone shoot him? Then events of the past few weeks started coming back to him. Someone from his violent past was trying to even the score by sabotaging his work-site in New Jersey. They were putting his business at risk. Now they were trying to kill him.

He started to worry. How would he protect his business if he was in a hospital? Jack was his second in command, but Jack knew nothing about the old days. He wouldn't be equipped to fight the saboteurs. Bob was in a stew. He must have been moaning because Jane became alarmed. She called the nurse.

The nurse wanted to know what the problem was. He told her everything was fine. She checked his vitals and finally left.

Jane held his hand. She tried to soothe his feelings. She squeezed his hand and said, "Honey, you need not to worry and get well. Jack, Mike and Paul have things under control just as you planned. Mike has the hospital locked down. A gnat can't get in here without his okay. Jack has taken over the business until you get well. Paul is working with Jack and Mike to find out who shot you."

That didn't give Bob a lot of comfort. He knew Jack wasn't equipped to find out who shot him and Mike and Paul wouldn't talk to Jack about the past without Bob's okay. Bob wasn't particularly worried about his safety. That was the last thing on his mind. It was the business and his family's wellbeing that worried him. He had developed Jack to take over the business in just this kind of scenario. However, the twist was this sabotaging. Bob hadn't planned on a scenario like that.

He asked for Jack. Jack was by his side. He didn't have enough energy to tell Jack what he wanted. He decided to stick with his plan. Jack was looking straight down into his face. Bob said, "Jack I trust you. You have my complete confidence. Do whatever you have to do."

The nurse and an assistant came in to move his bed to another room. This room was the recovery room and he was being moved to a regular room. On the way out of the room they passed a man by the door in a suit. Bob looked up at him, but he didn't recognize him. He did recognize the bulge under the guy's jacket. He was armed. He must be one of Mike's men.

In his new room Bob felt exhausted. He didn't know why since he had ridden to his room in a bed on wheels. They had many tubes going in and out of him. They were probably pumping meds into him through a tube. He drifted off to sleep.

13

Danny's Job

Mike came to my office as I requested. It was before normal business hours. We had talked in general terms on the plane coming back from Asheville, but now we needed to get down to specifics. I wanted to change our direction on investigating the sabotaging, and I needed Mike's support.

We got comfortable in the conference area of my office. I had coffee cake that I picked up from Momma's earlier in the morning. Mary brought in coffee. It was a special bean that I had ground fresh. I knew Mike liked it.

I did all of this to be polite to my friend. I knew it would have no effect on what he thought. Only my words would sway him.

"Mike, I asked you to come here because we need to take action. Our highest priority is Bob's safety. I believe that we have done everything possible in that area. Another high priority is to save his company. I need your cooperation in this regard."

"What can I do?"

"I strongly believe that we need to change directions on the New Jersey sabotaging. If we don't stop it immediately, the company is going down the tubes."

"Yeah, I know you think that. I have given it some thought. I think we should send Danny to New Jersey. He is an expert at setting up cameras for surveillance. Maybe we can catch the perps up to no good. It won't stop the next sabotaging, but it might tell us who is doing it, and then we can stop it. It might not tell us who is behind it, so it might not stop it permanently. That is why Bob was so focused on the 'old days'."

"Do you think Danny is the right guy?" I immediately regretted my question. Of course Mike thought that Danny was the right guy, or he wouldn't have recommended him. I apologized.

"No problem. I understand your concern. Danny is young, but he is good at surveillance. If he follows instructions, there will be no risk and no confrontation. His job will be to send pictures back."

"Okay. I agree. Let's set it up. When you and Danny are ready, let me know. I will have the company plane fly him and whomever else you want to New Jersey. This needs to be done right away. We need to stop this hemorrhaging."

"He's ready right now."

This meant Mike had listened to me on the plane and had anticipated my request. That made me feel a lot better. I didn't need to pressure Mike into following my directions.

"Okay, I will phone the company pilot. The plane will be ready to take off within the hour. Thanks for your help."

I felt a little relief that we were now doing the right thing. I knew it was late. We should have been doing this a long time ago. The thing is you can't change the past. You can only learn from the past and work toward the future.

I was confident that this was right, but there still was a risk from the past. Especially since Bob was shot. Somehow I didn't think the saboteurs would resort to shooting. It wasn't consistent. Maybe Bob knew more than I gave him credit for. If he knew something from the past, it would explain why he had taken no action in New Jersey. I voiced my concerns to Mike before he left. Mike felt that they had covered the bases on the past although there was one lead that bothered him, and he was still running it down. Most of the players were either dead or in prison. It didn't seem likely that they were behind this, but I was left feeling that we were missing something.

At any rate we had to stop the work slowdowns in New Jersey. We needed badly to keep that project on schedule and secure Bagotti's support.

14

The Sheriff I

The sheriff maneuvered his big belly under the steering wheel of his cruiser. Every time he did it he thought about going on a diet, and he always set the same time to do it—next week. His weaknesses were sugary drinks, snacks, and eating at Momma's. She was a great cook, and he had a great appetite. He always made sure he paid her. He never threw his weight as sheriff around. He snickered. He weighed too much to throw his weight around. It could hurt somebody. He figured treating people right was one of the things that kept him in office. He treated people with respect.

He was on his way over to the hospital to talk with Bob McAvoy. He had known Bob since they were kids. They grew up together. Bob was an aggressive guy in business and had turned a failed family coal company into a large construction company. That took a lot of doing and a lot of cash.

People had their theories on how Bob raised so much

cash in such a short time with no credit and no collateral. The sheriff had his own theory, but he kept it to himself. He liked to stick with facts, and he had no facts, just ideas. Also, Bob was a friend and a big campaign contributor.

His immediate problem was that Bob had been shot, and it was the sheriff's job to find out who did it. He had retrieved the bullet from the hospital. He would have it examined by the state police and checked against databases in case the weapon had been used in other crimes. It was a long shot, and the sheriff wouldn't take it for most people, but Bob wasn't most people.

The sheriff knew the bullet was a .223 caliber and probably from an AR-15 (Armalite Rifle - 15) rifle. That was like finding out it was a leaf from a tree. Still, it was a fact and accumulating facts was what investigation was all about.

The sheriff pulled into the hospital parking lot. He didn't park in a handicap spot or the employee parking like some cops might have done. He parked in the regular visitor parking lot.

It was a hike to the front door, which made him think about a diet again. The sheriff felt bad. He should take care of himself like Bob and his cronies do. They were all athletes, especially Jack Clayton.

Clayton was a giant. The sheriff bet that Clayton weighed close to two hundred and sixty-five pounds. The sheriff weighed more, but it was mostly fat. That made him think about his diet again. Clayton worked out like it was a job that paid well. He carried a lot of muscle and no fat.

He had appeared out of nowhere almost two years ago. He had come from Ohio, and the story was that his wife had divorced him and her family had driven him out of town. The sheriff was curious about Clayton, but he had no official reason to investigate him. Still, he ran a check on him in Ohio and found that his story checked out.

Strangely, Clayton had fallen in with Bob, Mike Randall and Paul Jackson. The four of them were like brothers. The sheriff had his suspicions about Bob, Mike and Paul. He had no proof, just suspicions. These suspicions carried over to Clayton. All of them were upstanding citizens, and the sheriff had no complaints. The sheriff believed that if you crossed any one of them, you might not live long. That was true of a lot of men in the mountains, but the difference with Bob and his friends was that you weren't going to catch them. They were a clever and careful group.

The sheriff knew Clayton fairly well because he and his deputies used the shooting range at The Cabin. Clayton managed The Cabin, but of course, it was McAvoy who actually gave the permission. It was a great shooting range, much better than anything the county could afford. He often saw other cops there. Sometimes it was like old home day.

Clayton sometimes came out to the range with them and shot handguns. He was a good shot.

The sheriff was often nervous around Clayton, and he wasn't exactly sure why. There was no reason for it. Besides he was the sheriff, not Clayton. Clayton was huge and strong as an ox. He sometimes helped Red at The Gin Mill with the rowdies. That was okay with the sheriff because it saved his guys from being called so often.

The sheriff suspected that Clayton was capable of killing. He might not be the killer that he thought McAvoy, Jackson and Randall were, but he seemed comfortable in that group. Birds of a feather tend to flock together.

Randall was a stone cold killer in the sheriff's opinion. Again he had no facts, but he could feel it. Jackson was quiet. The sheriff didn't know exactly what to think about him. As for McAvoy, the sheriff grew up with him. No one ever pushed McAvoy around and got away with it. McAvoy was a guy who you didn't mess with.

The sheriff was only a deputy when a kid raped Lydia Harding. Soon after that McAvoy, Jackson and Randall showed up on leave from the army. Coincidentally, the kid disappeared. He was allegedly seen driving south out of the county, and then McAvoy, Jackson and Randall went back to the army. The sheriff didn't believe in coincidences. There wasn't a shred of evidence, but the sheriff had his beliefs. The sheriff also believed that if justice was going on, why interfere?

The sheriff went in the front door and checked with the staff on Bob's location. He was sent to the elevator and up several floors. When he got to Bob's door, he noticed a man giving him the eye. He could see that the man was armed. He didn't recognize him, but he knew he was one of Randall's men. The sheriff had assigned deputies to security, but Randall had insisted on some of his own men. The sheriff was okay with that. It saved on his manpower of which he was short.

To be polite he stopped and introduced himself. They chatted briefly, and the sheriff went into Bob's room. It was the first time he had seen him after he was shot.

The sheriff was a little taken aback. Bob looked awful. His face was pale and drawn. He looked like death warmed over. Well, a good shooting will do that to you. It isn't like the movies or TV. Getting shot hurts, and you don't necessarily bounce back like a rubber ball.

The sheriff grabbed a chair and sat next to Bob's bed.

Then he saw that Bob couldn't turn his head to see him. He stood back up so that Bob could see him. It was awkward.

"So dude, I heard you got shot. What happened?"

"I don't have a clue."

"Don't you remember anything?"

"Nope. Nothing. The last thing I remember was driving down the highway. The next thing I knew, I was waking up in the recovery room."

The sheriff pondered this. He knew Bob was capable of spinning a very credible lie, but he had a feeling that Bob was telling the truth. In any case he knew he wasn't going to get any help from Bob.

It wasn't a big surprise. When coming to the hospital, he thought it would be a waste of investigative time. However, he had his official duty to perform, and he wanted to say hi to his old friend.

"Bob, you better get busy and get well. I am going to find the bastard who shot you. You can count on me to do just that."

* * *

Bob watched the sheriff leave. With the bed cranked up he could see the door. He still couldn't turn his head much, but he could see the door.

The sheriff was a good friend, and he was a good sheriff. Bob had supported him in every campaign. Plus, they had grown up together. But Bob knew the sheriff had about as much of a chance of catching his shooter as he would have skating across hell on roller-blades. Bob was sure it was a professional hit.

15
Danny II

Danny was beside himself with excitement. This was his first assignment on the road. He would be on his own. He had worked two years around the office hoping for an assignment like this one. It was an easy job. All he had to do was install some cameras and have the data send back to the office. Both Uncle Mike and Uncle Jack had impressed upon him the importance of the job. It made Danny proud that he could help his friends out.

Danny had studied electronics and, specifically, electronic surveillance in a community college. Uncle Mike had made that possible. He acted like a father to Danny. He guessed it was because Uncle Mike and Frankie had no children. Whatever the reason, it was a godsend to Danny who would have had no opportunities without Uncle Mike.

Frankie was a fox. No man could keep his eyes off her, but you had to do it with respect. If Uncle Mike suspected otherwise, you probably wouldn't live long or if you did, you were going to be in a lot of pain.

Danny had no first hand knowledge of Uncle Mike killing anyone, but there were rumors. Danny had studied him quite a bit and formed the opinion that He was capable of killing a man. Certainly in the army on Mr. McAvoy's team he must have killed. Uncle Mike, Mr. McAvoy, and Paul served together in special ops, but none of them ever spoke of what happened. He just knew that whatever happened Uncle Mike and Paul had a lot of respect for Mr. McAvoy, who at times they called Captain.

Now, Mr. McAvoy had been shot and was in the hospital. He knew Uncle Mike, Uncle Jack, and Paul were gearing up to catch the shooter. In Danny's opinion the shooter was going to die.

Uncle Jack was a case. Uncle Mike had a lot of respect for him and had introduced Danny to Uncle Jack at The Cabin. They formed a friendship. Uncle Jack let him use the firing range any time he wanted, and they often shot together. Uncle Jack was cool, and he was big as a mountain.

Thinking about Uncle Jack reminded him that there was another fox at The Cabin, Ms. Harding. She was another case. She was beautiful, but didn't like guys except for Uncle Jack. She really liked him. He was about the only guy Danny knew who was taller than Ms. Harding. She was very tall but still a fox. She always treated him in a friendly way. Maybe she wasn't afraid of him? Or maybe it was because Uncle Jack and he were friends. Danny was careful to call her Ms. Harding. Both Ms. Harding and Uncle Jack said he could call her Lydia, but he wanted to be careful. Just thinking about the size of Uncle Jack's fists made Danny sweat.

Danny had worked for Uncle Mike for two years after college. He worked in the office taking care of Uncle Mike's IT work and data protection. He liked his job, but it lacked the excitement that he hoped for. Danny was itching to get in on the security end of Uncle Mike's business and see action in the field.

So here he was on Mr. McAvoy's company plane alone, flying to New Jersey. He was going to make sure he didn't blow this assignment. He had spent hours making sure he had all the right equipment and that the equipment was working. He also had a plan in case the equipment didn't work. He had backups. He was ready.

He could feel the plane descending. The pilot told him to fasten his seatbelt. Danny could feel his toes tingling. This was it.

He got off the plane and collected his equipment. He had several boxes because of all the backups. Paul made sure that there was a van and a driver there to pick him up. The driver helped Danny load his equipment into the van, and they drove to the job site.

The foreman met them and took Danny on a tour, showing him where the sabotages had taken place. In short order Danny had a plan of where to put the cameras. He set up six cameras and had the software set up so he could upload the data to his laptop anytime he wanted. It would also be sent to the office automatically where it would be encrypted and archived, according to Uncle Mike's instructions. Danny planned on staying in New Jersey for one night or maybe two nights to make sure everything was working correctly. This was important, and he needed to make sure it went right.

At the same time he was anxious to get back to West Virginia to be with his new wife. He missed her.

16

Lights Out

On the second day in New Jersey Danny checked the camera data. The cameras were essentially the kind nature lovers use to catch pictures of wild animals, or tame animals if you want to know what your cat is doing at night, assuming your cat is tame. Danny smiled thinking of Lydia's cat, The Cat. That cat was only partially tame. Word had gotten around and most people were afraid of The Cat. Danny liked to think he wasn't afraid of The Cat, but he kept a sharp eye out when at The Cabin.

The only thing wrong was that there was no data because nothing triggered the cameras. Danny felt like a jerk on that one. He should have known this. Without any data he didn't know for sure if the cameras were working. He decided to stay a second night and to trigger the cameras himself. He could do it in the daytime, but nighttime was more realistic. He would go to the job site after dark and trigger all the cameras.

That night he parked near the office trailer where the workers parked. He figured his car would look like one of the workers had left their car there overnight. It had just gotten dark. It was perfect for checking the cameras. He would trigger all six, and then go back to his car to check the data.

When he got to the second camera, he heard the roar of motors. He knew the sound. It was a group of Harleys. The Harley sound was unmistakable. No other bike sounded like it. In fact, Harley Davidson tried to patent the sound. It was one of their trademarks.

Uncle Jack told him the joke. Harley Davidson saved money by not putting in an offset crankshaft. It had a V-twin motor with a straight crankshaft pin so the firing was uneven, giving it the unique sound. Other manufacturers used offset crankshafts for a smoother motor. So because of the cost savings, Harleys ended up with a unique sound. It became so popular that as an afterthought they tried to patent the sound.

Uncle Jack rode a Harley. Sort of. It was modified to be extra long. It was a sight. Uncle Mike, Mr. McAvoy and Paul rode Harleys as well.

Danny hid behind some machinery to see if he could see what was happening. The motors were shut off, and he heard talking. He couldn't hear well enough to understand what was being said. He moved closer to the talking. He still couldn't understand, so he moved closer.

The talking stopped. He waited. It was a hot night, and there were mosquitoes buzzing around. Danny had to ignore the bites. The noise of a slap might attract the attention of the bikers. The mosquitoes were loading up on his blood.

He wondered what the bikers were doing. It was quiet and that was disturbing. Especially after they had been talking. Patience is a virtual. He waited.

Suddenly, an arm from behind grabbed him. It was too quick for him to resist. He felt a sting and something warm on his neck. It was dark, but he was able to see lights in the distance. The lights started to fade, and then they went out. All was quiet.

17
Tears

Mike burst into my office like a run away bulldozer. Mary appeared in the doorway after Mike came in, giving me a look that said she was unable to stop him or had time to notify me he was coming in. I gave her a smile and signaled that everything was okay. Normally, she would offer to get us coffee, but she could see something was terribly wrong. She closed the door quietly and went back to her desk.

Mike sat down in front of me with tears running down his face. I was shocked to the core. Mike was a stone-cold killer, and no one had ever seen a tear in his eye unless it was Frankie in private.

Thinking of Frankie sent a chill over me. What if something had happened to Frankie? That could certainly cause this kind of reaction. I sat and waited for Mike to get himself together. When he did, I received totally unexpected news.

He said, "Danny was killed last night. They cut his

throat ear to ear, the bastards."

I could scarcely believe my ears. We had sent Danny to New Jersey to take photographs. How could that lead to his getting killed? Sabotage, Bob shot and now Danny was dead. What the hell was going on? I thought maybe Bob was right. This could be coming from his violent past.

Pangs of sadness stabbed through my chest. Danny was a good friend. We had spent a lot of time together hiking and shooting. I couldn't believe he was gone. Jesus, he just got married. I realized Mike was talking.

"What am I going to tell Bonnie? They were just married, and now he is dead. They will blame me. Was it my fault? Christ Jack, was it my fault?

"No Mike, it wasn't your fault. He was supposed to take pictures. That shouldn't have gotten him killed. Do you want me to notify Bonnie? Someone needs to tell her before this gets on the news."

"No, I need to let her know. It is my job. Jesus, I wish I could crawl under a rock."

I had never seen Mike so upset and so unstrung.

Also, I don't think I had ever heard so much swearing in my office before. I usually don't allow it.

I told him to get to Bonnie in person right away and then come back. We needed to make plans. Before he left he said he already had his crew going over the data captured the night before. He gave me the name of the lead guy, Jim.

I didn't know Jim. I gave him a call and introduced myself. He said he was expecting my call. Mike had prepared him. Jim said that they had good pictures and several showed the guy who cut Danny's throat. I didn't say anything to Jim, but I thought all we have to do is identify this guy in the photograph, and he is a dead man. If Mike didn't kill him, I would. That was right up there with things that you could count on, like gravity.

I hung up the phone and thought. The cops were going to be in this thing soon. They would want a crack at the killer. The problem with that was the killer would get a relatively light (in my opinion) sentence. I wanted him dead. We needed to be careful on how much data we gave the police. We could handle that. I would talk with Mike when he came back from notifying Bonnie.

The thought of Bonnie made me think of the funeral. A funeral had to be planned. I guessed that the family would want a funeral. That was traditional here in the mountains. The family would be responsible for the funeral, but Mike and I could make sure they had everything they needed. If they were upset with Mike, I might have to take care of that part.

I didn't know if Frankie, Bob, Jane, Paul, Liz and Lydia knew about this or not. I figured Mike should tell Frankie. I would tell Lydia, Jane, and Paul. Paul would tell Liz. Jane could tell Bob. She would know how to handle it. He was still in the hospital, and it had to be handled with care. I could tell her how much we knew, and she could take it from there.

Lydia would need support. She liked Danny and would need me around her. She was still reeling from Bob's being shot. I couldn't leave the office because Mike was coming back, and I needed to talk with Paul. I could have Lydia come to my office. Then I realized what a stupid idea that was. Where was my brain when I needed it? I had to go to The Cabin to be with Lydia. Mike and Paul could find me there. I texted both of them, and told them I was headed for The Cabin.

I didn't dare tell Mary, my assistant, yet because she would tell everyone she knew. Danny was well liked, and this news would spread like wildfire. I needed to wait until Mike talked with Danny's wife and family. That would be at least an hour. I told her there was an emergency, and I would fill her in as soon as I could. I left for The Cabin.

I found Lydia in my office working on her contract. She could see right away something awful had happened.

She exclaimed, "Is it Bob? Has his condition worsened?"

"No, Lydia, Bob is okay. It's Danny. He was killed last night. His throat was cut." Thinking back on it I could probably have left the throat cutting part out.

Lydia screamed, "No!" and bust into tears. I walked around the desk and held her. I felt hot tears in my eyes, but I had work to do.

As Lydia got control of herself she asked, "What happened? I thought he was on a routine assignment doing some photographing."

"He was. We don't know exactly what happened."

She thought about it and then asked, "Who knows? Has everyone been notified?"

I said, "No. Mike is notifying Bonnie and her family as we speak. After I hear back from Mike, I am going to call Jane, and she will notify Bob. I will call Paul, and he will notify Liz. I assume that Mike will notify Frankie. I will notify Mary as soon as the others know, and that will take care of the rest of the community. I came back to The Cabin to be with you, but I need to get a lot of things going. I will need my office, or I will have to go back to my business office."

"I don't want to be alone at the moment. Please stay here. I can leave the office if you have something confidential to talk with someone about."

I stayed. Mike came to my Cabin office. He brought Frankie with him so she could be with Lydia. Frankie hugged Lydia. Both were crying. They went off to be with each other.

Mike and I got things rolling. Paul showed up, and we made plans. We needed to find Danny's killer, Bob's shooter and stop the sabotages. We had things started, but there was a lot to do.

We also had social duties. We had to see that Bonnie was supported in this terrible time, and there was the funeral.

God, the funeral. I was still raw from burying my son. It had been less than a year, and those things generate deep feelings that take a long time to settle. My son was just a little boy. Danny had just cleared his adolescence. It is tragic when the young die. One misses them, and you can't help but think about all the years that they were cheated out of.

18

The Funeral

Danny's funeral was coming up like a bad storm. You know it is going to be terrible, but there is nothing you can do about it. You grit your teeth and tough it out.

It was less than a year ago that I attended my son's funeral. The only support I had were The Club members. I had been forced out of my family less than a year prior to Will's funeral. I was put in the unusual position of offering condolences to my ex-wife and her family, but only my West Virginia friends offered me condolences.

Lydia was especially supportive in a quiet way. She stayed by my side with the loyalty of a dedicated friend, which was a little strange because at the time I didn't think of us as friends. Looking back on it I can see that maybe we were friends. During the hardest part of the ordeal, Lydia slid her arm under my arm and held on. I found it comforting.

I was hoping to have the same arrangement this time,

but it was not to be. I was one of the pallbearers and had to sit in the front of the church with Mike and the rest of the pallbearers. I had a great urge to turn around to catch Lydia's eye, but I knew it wouldn't look right. I stared straight ahead like Mike was doing.

There was a viewing in the funeral home before going to the church. People were solemn, and there was a seemingly endless stream of people. Old people often die alone, but young people still have friends and family. Danny was well liked, and it seemed that everyone who knew him was at the viewing, paying their respects. It isn't natural to bury one so young.

The funeral director, or at least his staff, had done a wonderful job in fixing Danny up so an open casket was possible. Still Danny looked like a corpse. I have never liked looking at dead people in viewings. To me they always look like dead people with makeup, which of course is what they are.

The family requested that donations be made to a fund for Danny's wife in lieu of flowers. Many people chose to do both, and the casket was surrounded with flowers. Lydia and I bought a flower arrangement, and I donated heavily to Danny's fund for his wife.

Some people feel that the flowers are wasted at a funeral because they are used a few minutes, and then discarded. I have a different view. I think flowers at a funeral serve a valuable function even if it is brief. The flower arrangement around the casket made it much more acceptable to me.

After the viewing hours, the funeral director's staff escorted the people out to their cars for the trip to the church. We pallbearers were requested to stand by the casket and view the body as the director covered Danny's face with the casket blanket and closed the lid. We then took the casket to the hearse. We loaded the flowers into a car to be taken to the church. Afterward some of the flowers would be taken to the hospital and some to a nursing home. I requested that our flowers stay on Danny's grave. I think a newly closed grave without flowers is sad. It is better for me if there are some flowers on the grave.

The funeral was held in the same church as Danny

and Bonnie's wedding. It seemed cruel that only a few weeks ago we were in this building for a happy occasion and now such a sad occasion. Weddings and funerals are two milestones in a person's life, and one would like to have them separated by many happy years. Danny and Bonnie were cheated of this.

There was not a dry face in the crowd. There was a lot of sobbing. A more heart wrenching scene could not be found. It is one of the moments when you question God and people. Why does God allow such things to happen? Why do people do such things?

It is one thing to attend a funeral of a friend or relative advanced in years. It is a sad time, but not unexpected. We grieve for ourselves because but for the snap of the fingers of fate we think there go I. We grieve because we miss the person. We grieve for a thousand reasons. But when a young person dies, we grieve for life itself. How can such a thing happen? Where was God when this happened? It is a shock to our system. Our stability is shaken. It tests our notion of life. It is unfair. It has broken some kind of unwritten rule. We question whether we know how to go on. How can we live if we don't know the rules?

The funeral was mercifully short. There is no point in dragging out a funeral. It shouldn't be too long or too short. It needs to be respectful but not dwelt upon. The minister did a competent job with the words and the timing.

He talked about how the body in the casket was not the real Danny. Danny's soul was already in the heavens above. He said we all should take comfort in that fact. I thought the believers were so lucky. They can be comforted by this idea. I am not a believer, and it was not a comfort to me. To me Danny had died a needless death, and he was gone. His candle flame of life had been extinguished to burn no more.

It was a heavy task carrying Danny's body from the church to the hearse and then to his grave. It is such a final act.

The interment service was brief. After it, the funeral director hit the switch and the casket began its slow descent. That is a heart wrenching few minutes. It drove home the notion that Danny was making his last trip on this earth. Most of the people were moving away, but I stayed until his casket was fully in the grave.

Everyone had been invited to The Cabin for a meal donated by friends and relatives. Normally, such events are held in a community house, but there were a lot of people and food service would be easier at The Cabin with our large kitchen. Probably most of the people were anxious to get away from the cemetery and get to a happier place.

Before I left the cemetery, I said a prayer over Danny's grave. I felt Lydia's hand on my arm, and I sensed Mike and Frankie nearby. Out of the corner of my eye I saw Paul and Liz standing with us. I am not a religious guy, but in front of God I promised Danny that his killer would die. I heard Mike and Paul say amen. Lydia whispered amen.

19

The Sheriff II

The sheriff went to the funeral. He had met Danny at The Cabin shooting range, but he didn't know him well. It seemed like everyone went to his funeral. It was a big crowd of people, a lot of voters. The sheriff wore a suit in place of his uniform, but he wore a gun under his coat. Unfortunately, one can't predict when such a tool is needed.

When a young person dies, people search for answers. How is it that such a young person dies? Why is that? The older generations ask themselves, "What if this were my son?" They go to the funeral out of respect for the family and for life itself. People want comfort.

The sheriff hoped that they found comfort. He personally found none in the funeral. To him Danny's killing was a waste, and the funeral wasn't going to help him. The funeral did help the family and friends. The sheriff prayed for the family. It broke his heart to think of Danny's widow. They had been married just a few weeks.

The sheriff was thankful that Danny wasn't killed in his jurisdiction. The sheriff had enough to worry about without having to find out who killed Danny. As it was, he was working on who shot McAvoy. That was an active investigation without a lot of clues. The sheriff had his theory of who did it, but he kept it to himself because he had no evidence. He was working on it though, and one of these days the case was bound to break.

The sheriff was acutely aware that people didn't think he would solve the case. One person in particular who was skeptical was Bob McAvoy. The sheriff was good friends with Bob, but he felt that Bob viewed him as a hillbilly with limited investigative skills. Well, the sheriff was a hillbilly. So what? He could still figure out puzzles. Plus, he wanted very badly to arrest the person who shot his boyhood friend.

The sheriff started with the question: Who wanted Bob McAvoy dead? If you knew that, you probably knew who shot him. The sheriff knew that Bob thought it was someone from the old days. The sheriff privately agreed, but he was thinking in a different direction from Bob. The minister said something that brought the sheriff back to the present, back to the funeral.

The church was packed. They had extra chairs set up in the foyer, and there were a few people standing. Even more people had showed up at the viewing. It was a steady stream of people.

It was painful watching the relatives and friends of Danny seeing off one so young. The sheriff had to deal with young death occasionally due to car wrecks, so it wasn't new to the sheriff. Going to the funeral was new. He could hardly escape it with so much of the community attending the funeral. His was an elected position, so he had to keep up appearances. That was one angle. The other thing was that he knew Danny and liked him. Everybody who knew Danny liked him.

Afterward almost everyone went to The Cabin. Other than the donated food it was a typical McAvoy event although he probably didn't plan it since he was still in the hospital.

The Cabin was an amazing place. It was a combination resort and armed compound. He knew how much security Mike had installed, and he knew about the guns and ammo in the basement. He shot at Bob's range like the rest of the cops in the area.

It was a great party with lots to eat, but he left early to go to the hospital to see Bob. He looked a lot better. He was able to turn his head some and his color was more normal.

He chatted with Bob a few minutes but didn't mention the investigation. He didn't want to stress Bob, and besides he didn't think Bob was able to help and maybe not willing.

Bob asked him how the investigation was going, but the sheriff knew he just was being polite. He could sense Bob's low expectation of him. That bothered the sheriff for a number of reasons. Primarily, he wanted his friend's respect.

He was going to solve this case if it was the last thing he did on this earth. He needed a break. He needed some evidence.

20

Bob's Longest Trip

Bob had just completed what he thought was the longest trip of his life. He was soaked in sweat. The pain of walking was excruciating, and he was as weak as a newborn kitten. It took all the stamina that he could muster to make the trip. He had just gone to the bathroom.

How is it that in the movies the protagonist is able to get out of bed and move around with impunity after receiving major injuries or surgery? It probably makes the movie better. Bob was facing real life and it hurt like the dickens.

He thought he was going to pass out from the pain, and he was no wimp. He had endured pain, exhaustion, disappointment, and untold hazards in the military. True, he had never been shot in the military. This time he had been shot, and the surgeons had to do major surgery to remove the bullet and repair the damage. He had almost bled to death in the ambulance and during surgery.

Maybe that was why he was so weak. His trip to the bathroom showed him just how long his recovery was going to be, and that was depressing.

He was needed on the job. His company was at risk of failure if they didn't get things under control soon. Bob was sure their problems were coming from the old days when he, Paul, Mike and some others raised cash by robbing drug dealers. It was a dangerous business, but it was the only way that Bob could raise the needed cash to save the family business. That was all history. The business was fully legitimate now, but Bob was worried that someone from his past was bent on revenge.

He knew that Jack disagreed with this line of reasoning and with Bob's directions, but Jack didn't know Bob's past. Jack didn't know how violent and vengeful these men were.

Bob also suspected that Mike sided with Jack. That worried him because Mike was very levelheaded. Bob wasn't quite sure what Paul thought. Paul kept his opinions to himself and tended to defer to Bob's rank.

Well, all of this was on hold for the moment. By previous arrangement, Jack would be running the business until Bob could function, and it looked like that was going to be a while. Bob had to at least be able to go to the bathroom by himself.

Going to the bathroom unassisted was one of the major criteria for him to be released from the hospital, a primary goal at the moment. He had therefore forced himself to get out of bed and push his walker to the bathroom in his room. He did his business and made it back to his bed.

For a while he thought the nurse wasn't going to let him flush so she could check on him. She was as strict as an old time schoolmarm. He liked her, and they got along fine. He didn't mind people being strict when they were doing their job. In fact, he liked it.

When they first met after his surgery, she was a stranger. They had gotten to know each other in the ensuing days. She was a professional, but she also had a curiosity of who he was. The armed security at his door naturally attracted her attention. No one had been under her care with an armed guard before. Also, normally people were not allowed in a patient's room outside of visiting hours, but people visited him anytime they wanted. From all this she knew Bob had connections, and he was someone who others wanted dead.

Her questions were carefully and politely constructed, but Bob figured out that she wanted to know if he was a gangster. That amused Bob. He never thought of himself as a gangster, but the more he thought about it, the more he realized that he used to be one. He told her, no, he was just a businessman and sometimes they made enemies.

She didn't demand to inspect the results of his trek to the bathroom. Maybe she was afraid of him, but somehow he didn't believe that.

The important thing was that he made it. By the time he got back into bed he was exhausted. She came into the room to check on him. She could probably see from his condition that he had made to the bathroom. She smiled. It was a rare event. She seemed pleased that he had made his historic trip to the john. He got more or less comfortable, and with the help of meds, he dropped off to sleep.

21
The Video

Mike, Paul and I met in my business office. Mike had a report on the cameras. The biker gang found three cameras and destroyed them. Three other cameras were intact, but they didn't capture the event.

Danny was a professional. He had the system programmed so that as soon as a camera sensed motion, it automatically captured the video and sent the data home. We therefore had video to view. The New Jersey cops had the empty cameras.

Mike popped a CD into my office TV. The picture was dark, but you could see images. Danny appeared in the frame. He turned to his left. He either heard something, or he was just looking around. As he turned, a man appeared behind Danny and slipped his arm around him. The man jerked his arm back. Danny reached for his throat and collapsed. We had just seen Danny die. With the power of electronics, we could watch Danny die as many times as we wished. I didn't want to watch. It was stomach churning, but we needed the information.

Mike's staff had captured the picture of the man, enhanced it, and enlarged it. We had a photograph of the man who killed Danny. We needed to identify the man and learn everything there was to be known about him. What did he do for a living? Who were his friends? Where did he hang out? Did he have a family? Did he belong to a club? How old was he? Everything.

Mike wanted to personally go to New Jersey and do the legwork. Both Paul and I disagreed. It could take a few weeks, and we needed Mike here to take care of Bob's security. Also, we still needed find Bob's shooter, and Mike was the lead on that effort.

Paul was probably the most rational guy in the room. Both Mike and I were emotionally tied to Danny. I could see that Paul had an idea. I looked at him, and he said, "I think we should get Snake on the job. No one is better at gathering this kind of data than Snake."

I had met Snake briefly in the southwest when we were searching for my kidnapped son. Snake is a hardcore biker and a drug dealer. Ordinarily, you would want to keep a respectable distance between you and Snake except for one thing: He is a genius at reconnaissance. He had located where my son was taken.

Like Bob, Paul, and Mike, he got his training in the military. Snake was on Bob's special ops team along with Paul and Mike. There was a solid trust between them forged in blood.

Mike spoke up, "How are we going to contact Snake? No one has his phone number or address, if he has one."

Paul had already thought of this and said, "I'll have Bob give me his contact info. Bob will do it under the circumstances."

We mulled this over a few minutes. Bob was still an invalid. He wasn't able to go to Danny's funeral. The doctors told us to keep all stress away from Bob. However, this was an emergency, and we knew Bob would want to help. If we didn't ask him, and he found out later, he would be angry. We agreed to go ahead.

Paul would approach Bob and get the contact info for Snake.

22
Snake

Snake was just getting out of the shower when he heard his phone ring. It was his personal phone and very, very few people had the number. He wrapped a towel around himself and grabbed the phone. It was his sister. He was mildly alarmed. The chance of getting a phone call from her was about the same as a snow blizzard happening in south Florida.

"Hey kid, what's happening?"

"Someone by the name of Paul phoned me. He said that he is a friend of Captain, and he needs your help."

"Okay. Cool. How have you been doing?"

"I'm okay, but I'm at work, and I need to go."

There was a click, and the phone went dead. She was the only family Snake had. Everyone else had died. She was a citizen. She had a regular job, paid taxes, maybe even voted.

Snake on the other hand didn't do any of those things. Snake was a bad egg, and he knew it. It was how life broke for him. He was injured in the army, and the pain was bad, so they gave him pain meds. They were opiates, and he got hooked. One thing led to another and Snake ended up in prison. That was a bad scene, and he decided to turn things around. It was a painful process, but he had gotten himself off drugs.

Once out of prison, he went back to being a drug dealer, but he didn't use them himself. It was hugely profitable for Snake. He ran it just like a business except for details like taxes. He had a plan to make a lot of money and retire. There was big money to be made in drugs.

The U.S. government declared war on drugs. It was one of the dumbest things Snake had heard. Apparently, no one had learned a thing from Prohibition. The only thing Prohibition did was make millionaires out of bums, and today they would be multimillionaires. When there is a big market for a commodity, and the government makes that commodity illegal, it creates a free-for-all for people to get in on the profits. Instead of alcohol it is now drugs. And since it is illegal, you don't have to worry about stockholders and a lot of other things that legitimate businesses are stuck with. Your only worries are getting caught, ripped off, killed or having the IRS on your back.

Mexico had figured out the drug business. Mexico is a country without a lot of assets or natural resources. It has people who can work, and it has a decreasing supply of oil to export. For a while putting the people to work was a good deal, but then U.S. companies found that the Asians would work for even less, and the jobs went to Asia.

Mexico has another great asset. It sits on the border of one of the biggest drug markets in the world, the U.S. When people see a big market, the reasonable thing to do is to feed the market and make money. Mexico became a big drug exporter. Since it is illegal, no one knows for sure how big the business is, but clearly it is in the billions. It is probably Mexico's second biggest source of income or maybe even the largest.

When the U.S. declared war on drugs, Mexico was asked to help. Mexico wanted to be a good neighbor, so they promised to help, but why should they wipe out one of their most lucrative businesses? A lot of Mexican families depend on the drug jobs for support. Understandably, the results have not met expectations. The war on drugs is a huge failure and will remain so as long as the market exists.

Snake had thought this through. He joined the drug business. Where else can a felon earn millions?

His sister didn't see it this way. She thought the drug business was bad and that Snake might be killed or end up in prison again. She might be right, but his die had been cast.

His sister was the only person in this world who Snake loved. He knew she loved him, too.

Well, c'est la vie as they say in France. Snake took French in high school. He never used it much. In the army he had to learn two languages other than English as part of his job. Fortunately, Spanish was one of them. It helped him in the drug business.

Snake dialed the number his sister gave him. Paul answered. He was shocked to learn that Captain had been shot. Captain was a civilian now, and it was a mystery as to who would want to shoot him. Years ago it would have made sense but not now. Maybe it was random violence. It happens. However, Captain was shot with a .223 caliber. That didn't sound random.

Paul wanted him to do some surveillance work in New Jersey. Snake had never been in New Jersey. Well, that wasn't exactly true. He had flown in and out of the Newark airport a few times.

The surveillance involved a biker gang. That was cool. He was a biker and could fit in like a finger in a glove. It could be a lot of fun, if he didn't get killed. Bikers are very suspicious of outsiders, and if the stranger is suspected of being an informer, he disappears, as in goodbye forever.

Snake knew the rules. He also knew that if someone was going to kill him, they had better be good at it, or they would die first. Snake was no pushover. Snake had made his bones a long time ago and a few more wouldn't matter to him. Shoot first and the heck with the questions.

He made arrangements to maintain his business while he was gone. He bought airline tickets, using an alias and a stolen credit card. He figured he could be gone as long as a month. That would be no problem because he had a good team doing the day-to-day work. He could trust them more or less because they knew what would happen if they stole from him. A guy had tried it once, and he was found in pieces in a car. Snake had done that for the message, and it had worked. Down deep most people don't want to die and especially in a painful way. Most people want to live to old age and then sleep a very long time. You aren't going to do that if you steal from Snake.

Snake's assignment was to infiltrate a biker gang and learn the identity of the guy who killed a kid who was doing work for Captain. That was all fine and dandy, but you don't just walk into a biker gang's hangout and start chatting. You would probably have your head handed to you or at least your butt.

He needed a plan. He thought it over and realized that this could be a great business move. He would play the role of a drug dealer from the Midwest, looking for new markets. Except it wouldn't be playing a role. It would be the real deal. With any luck he would land a new customer as well as get the data Captain needed.

The more Snake thought about it the more he thought it was a stroke of genius. He was closer to Mexico than they were, and he had the connections in Mexico to get all the drugs he could market.

This also solved the problem of how to leave after the Captain's job was done. He actually wasn't going to leave. He would be their supplier and could drop in anytime. This plan gave him an entrance and eliminated the need for an exit. It was perfect.

He needed two things. The first was a business plan for dealing with these guys. He had to figure out how to get the drugs from Mexico to New Jersey without getting caught, and he needed to figure out the finances, so he could reap a healthy profit.

Second, he needed to make sure they never suspected him of being a spy or having anything to do with the elimination of the guy who killed the kid. He knew that one or more of the biker gang was going to die. That was the whole point of him scoping the scene out, right? If Snake disappeared right after one or more of the gang was killed, they might make the connection of his role. This is where his not leaving was so important. It was brilliant.

Snake might or might not have a direct role in eliminating the dude, but in any case he needed to make sure there was no connection to him. He didn't want to get killed, and he didn't want his business plan to be ruined. It would be like threading a needle made of dynamite. A slight slip and boom! Is life cool or what?

23

Bob Leaves the Hospital

Among all the bad news was some good news. Bob was doing well in the hospital. In fact, he was doing so well they said he could leave. The whole Club and his family were excited. The big question though was where he was going?

None of us thought that it was good for him to go home. First, we had not identified his shooter, so we needed to have Bob in a secure environment when there was another attempt on his life.

Second, his home was a two-story house, and Bob was far from being able to use stairs. In fact, he could hardly walk and only short distances with a walker. Stairs were out of the question.

We talked it over, and decided the best place would be The Cabin. It was set up for good security. Over the years Mike had wired the place with many sensors located in various places around the property. The Cabin was also easily defended. We could put guards in strategic places. The only worry was our guests. It wouldn't be good for the rental business if we had a gun fight at The Cabin. People are sensitive about those things.

The Cabin is a three-story building counting the basement, but it has an elevator. Bob could move around The Cabin in a wheelchair on any floor and out on the patio to get sun. It would be the best place.

Knowing Bob, he would probably have an electric wheelchair. I hoped he didn't leave tire skid marks on the floors while zooming around.

We made the arrangements for transportation from the hospital to The Cabin. We would move Bob in an ambulance. We got two ambulances and had a second guy dressed up to look like Bob. A shooter would not be able to tell which ambulance Bob was in. I felt like we were being a little paranoid, but Bob had been shot once, so we knew there was someone out there who wanted him dead.

We made sure the hospital told no one that Bob was leaving the hospital. Most people didn't know about it, and we wanted to keep it that way.

As with most security moves, everything went smoothly, and we never knew if we were just lucky, or if our precautions paid off. In this business you can only do your best and be glad that no one gets hurt.

We got Bob settled in his apartment at The Cabin. Jane was with him, but we also hired a nurse to help temporarily until Bob could do more for himself. Also Paul, Liz, Mike and Frankie moved into The Cabin for additional help and security for a few weeks.

Bob and Jane have a large three bedroom apartment with one bedroom set up as an office. We took their bed down and set up a hospital bed for Bob. Jane would sleep in the next bedroom. There was an intercom, so Jane could contact us at anytime for help. Bob couldn't get to the intercom, but he could call on his cell phone.

We would have communal meals, which made it more enjoyable. Liz, Frankie and Lydia set up to help with the meals. Lydia was a surprise in this department. When I first met her, she ate mostly peanut butter sandwiches because she couldn't cook. With my tutelage she had learned to be a good cook, but so far with a limited menu. She is a fast learner.

Mike took care of security. No one could get near The Cabin without setting off an alarm. In addition, Mike posted guards. All this security here and in New Jersey was costing us a fortune. As a CPA I could visualize all the money flowing out. I hoped that we could resolve this situation before we went broke. It seemed we were damned if we did and damned if we didn't. Without the security we could lose everything and with it we might end up broke.

With all of us living in The Cabin, there wasn't as much room to rent so that was cutting into our revenue. In these situations you just have to set priorities and stick to them. Make plans to support the priorities and work your plans. It was nerve wracking.

It would have been better if we knew who the shooter was, but that is life. On the better news side, we had had no more sabotaging since we had increased security at the job site. Once again we didn't know if our security measures were paying off, or if the saboteurs were scared off by Danny's murder investigation. In any case, the lack of new sabotaging had helped our business situation. We were back on schedule.

The local cops were on the scene in New Jersey investigating Danny's murder. They were a little handicapped. They didn't have as much data as we had. They demanded the video from our cameras, but they were told that that bikers destroyed cameras and data, which was partly true. We gave them the empty cameras. We wanted the killer to ourselves.

We were waiting for Snake to give us the information we needed to plan our next move. He had been on site in New Jersey for more than a week. It was time that we received a full report.

24

The Rock II

I had been doing a lot of thinking. I had been living in The Cabin and was an Officer-of-the-Club for about a year and a half. Until recently it was a good life. I had grown to the like other Officers-of-the-Club. I had even become good friends with Mike who at one time wanted to kill me.

I studiously avoided women in spite of plenty of offers. I am not a bad looking guy, and I have a body that a lot of women like. I used to take interest in that, and I found that there were three kinds of women: women who like big men, women who are afraid of big men, and those who don't care one way or the other. The first group is too clingy. The second group runs away. I like the third group, that is, if I were liking women.

After my painful divorce and losing my family, I was in no mood for a redo. I was steering away from women, at least for the time being.

One exception was Lydia. She was nearby, and I was

lonely. Eating by myself was when I missed my family the most. I could not, would not eat alone. I usually ate at Momma's Restaurant during the week. On weekends and during the summer when Lydia was at The Cabin, I invited her to eat with me. To me it was just a way of not being alone. In fact, I didn't even like her.

We spent a lot of time together. I guess I felt it was safe since I didn't like her. It sounds like a contradiction, and maybe it is, but I felt comfortable around her because I didn't like her. I knew there was no risk of involvement. What made it even better was the fact that she didn't like me. We made a good pair.

All of this worked until my son was kidnapped and killed. She came to the funeral in Ohio. After the funeral she manipulated things so she could ride back to The Cabin with me. Then on top of that, she invited me into her apartment for wine and food. That astonished me because prior to that no one ever went into her apartment. She even did her own plumbing and electrical repairs. Not even Bob was allowed in her apartment, and he owned the place. It made me think about our relationship.

I noticed that whenever the gang decided to do something, they always assumed that we would participate as a couple.

Lydia seemed okay with this as long as it wasn't called a date. She was adamant about not dating. That was okay with me although it tended to confirm my belief that she was crazy as a bedbug.

Bob required me to have a partner for our business functions in The Cabin. Since I didn't know any women that fit the bill, he made me bring Lydia. Much to our surprise, both Lydia and I enjoyed it. Lydia made sure it was known that it was just business.

I added up all the things I had observed. I was invited into her apartment. She stopped carrying her handgun when coming to dinner. We had fun dancing together. We enjoyed running together and taking walks in the woods. When uncomfortable or when she thought I needed support, she hung onto my arm like a life jacket at sea. Not only that, I liked it when she did it. What was a guy to make of all of this?

On sober reflection, I thought we needed to discuss it. I decided to invite her to The Rock. A rock that incidentally had become Our Rock.

It was the weekend, but she was in my office working on a contract. That was another thing. She used my home office for almost all her work. The only time she went to her apartment was when she slept. And now that I thought about it I remembered a few times when she fell asleep in my apartment and stayed the night on the sofa. She had a key to my apartment because of The Cat. She wanted to be able to come into my apartment and get The Cat if I was not around. So she came and went as she pleased.

I went to my office and asked her if she wanted to take a break. She agreed, and off we went.

I was nervous on the way to The Rock, and we didn't talk. We got to The Rock, climbed up and sat down. It was then when I realized what a bad idea it was to bring up the thing on my mind. I kept my mouth shut.

Lydia sat there for a while. Her hand slid under my arm, hugging my bicep. Then out of the blue she asked,

"What is bothering you?"

"What makes you think something is bothering me?"

"You asked me to come out here. You have been nervous, and you haven't talked. That means something is bothering you."

Trapped. That's the price you pay for hanging around a smart woman. I had no way to go but forward, and I said, "I thought we ought to discuss our relationship."

"What relationship are you talking about?"

"Well, I have been thinking about things, and I have come to a conclusion. When I came here, I vowed to not get involved with a woman, but I think things have spun out of control."

I took her hand and said, "I think I am in love with you."

Surprisingly, she didn't tense up. She didn't run away. She just sat there unmoved. I wondered if she heard me. Or maybe she was shocked into a catatonic state. I thought about having to do CPR. I didn't know what to do or say.

Finally, she said, "What makes you think that?"

I reviewed my observations with her. She listened patiently without comment.

In the end, she said that she thought the same thing although it was hard for her to know for sure because of her background. She admitted to having strong feelings for me.

I told her how she had sent a tingling up my spine more than one time. She giggled. I had never heard her giggle before. It was a happy sound. She turned to me, and I kissed her passionately. She returned the kiss. I felt that tingle from my head to my toes.

The last two years had been very rough years. This was the first true happiness I had had. We were like two teenagers in love. Love makes you feel young.

25

Snake's Report

It had been a couple of weeks since we sent Snake to New Jersey. We were getting reports from him, but they were too sketchy to act on. We were getting anxious for results.

I was in my home office wrapping up some work related emails. Lydia had been using my home office, but she usually worked in the daytime. This was in the evening, and I had the office to myself. I was on my last email when my phone rang. It was one of my throwaway phones. I would use it once and destroy it.

I answered, and it was Snake. He is a professional, but I could hear the excitement in his voice.

He had partially infiltrated the biker gang in question. He was hanging out with them in a bar, but he wasn't privy to all their talk. He had identified Danny's killer by name and had obtained personal data on him. The killer didn't have a regular residence, but he met with the gang leader every Wednesday night at the leader's house. There was a third guy who met with them. Snake determined that all three were part of the killing. They seemed to be the core of the gang.

The leader's house was in a rural area with no nearby neighbors. It was a wood-frame house on a large piece of land. The house was set back from the road with a long, straight drive from the road to the house. There was a small ridge behind the house. Each side of the house was clear for approximately a thousand feet.

The ridge was clear of trees so anyone crossing the ridge could be spotted easily. There was no way of approaching the house without being seen. The house had been selected with care.

Snake being Snake had taken photographs of the house. He would encrypt them and send them to us.

The biker gang was not large, but it had a reputation for being vicious. Most of them had prison records according to what Snake could gather from the bar talk.

Some of the gang members worked regular jobs, but several depended upon criminal activities for income. They were into drugs but were small time, which seemed to excite Snake. As he talked I realized he was planning a drug deal with the gang.

I didn't care what Snake did for a living, but I wanted nothing to interfere with our current project. I wasn't sure how to bring this up with Snake. There are some things you don't discuss when you are skirting the law, or, in this case, outright breaking the law. I didn't want to confront him about a potential drug deal.

I said, "Snake, nothing can interfere with the current project. I mean nothing. We have to have total concentration on this."

"I am with you. I understand, but you see I needed a way into this gang and a way out. It is my life on the line. A drug deal is the perfect ruse."

This made sense to me, and I felt better understanding what he was up to. He could have his drug deal as long as we got the guys who killed Danny.

"Thanks, Snake. I understand. I assume that this is your last report, and we will get a plan together. I'll get back with you when I know what we are going to do. Don't forget to send the photographs."

"Hey, you're talking to a professional. I never forget things on the job. You'll have the photographs in a few minutes."

"Sorry, I didn't mean to insult you. It is just that some of the people I work with are often forgetful of my instructions."

"You should have me train them. Probably take only one lesson."

"Different world, Snake."

"Yeah, I know. I'll see you later."

That was the longest conversation I ever had with Snake. I think it was because we were at a turning point. The reconnaissance was over. The action was about to begin.

26

The Plan

Mike, Paul and I met in my work office. We decided to use it because it had been recently swept for electronic bugs. We met in the evening when Mary Hatfield was not around. That meant I had to make the coffee.

That wasn't a big deal. Like with a lot of cooking you just have to follow the instructions. The problem though is that instructions often leave out critical steps or use cryptic shorthand, and there is skill involved. That isn't a problem with coffee. The machine is automatic. You put in water and the grounds and press the button for coffee. The secret is using the right grounds. I get a gourmet, fresh ground coffee and it is excellent.

Paul showed up first. We made small talk, waiting for Mike. Paul amazes me. No matter what, he is calm. I wondered how? Does he have a different body chemistry? Is he put together differently? It has to be something like that. It isn't just discipline although he has plenty of that as well. I think some people are just physiologically different. I wondered if Liz ever made him act excited. I hoped so. If not, they have a boring marriage.

Mike walked in and interrupted my musings. Probably a good thing. No matter how many times I have seen Mike enter a room, it still impresses me how he resembles a bulldozer. He isn't tall, but he is thick, and he often has a look on his face like a person who has determined to go through a wall head first, and has just made up their mind to do it. The only exception to this is when he is around Frankie. She has a big effect on him. She has a big effect on all men.

I got Mike a cup of coffee and warmed up Paul's and mine. I set out a dish of cookies. We were ready to start our discussion on how to take out the guys who killed Danny.

We had all reviewed the photographs of the leader's house and Snake's reports. There were two things that were crystal clear: The house was unapproachable without being seen, and the killer was hard to approach alone. Plus, we wanted to kill all three guys who were involved in killing Danny. It was hard and dangerous to kill three connected guys serially. You have to kill all three simultaneously. If you kill one, the others are wary and almost impossible to get near. But to kill all three together is not easy. I asked for ideas.

Paul was our planning guy. He had nothing. Mike had nothing. I had an idea.

My idea took advantage of all the disadvantages. My plan required that the three of them be together in an isolated spot. This happened every Wednesday night. My plan was a little unusual, but I thought it would work. To do it safely would require the contacts that Mike, Paul and Bob had, especially Bob. We didn't want to involve Bob, so I hoped that Paul or Mike could take care of the contacts.

I said, "I have an idea. We will blow them up on a Wednesday night."

I saw a slight smile cross Paul's lips. Mike looked at me like I had told him that not only was the Earth flat, but it was also square.

Paul was the first to speak, "How would we get a bomb into that house?"

"We use a truck."

Mike snickered just a little, letting me know how he felt, and then asked, "Who is going to drive the truck? It would be a suicide mission."

"We use a remotely controlled truck."

There were puzzled looks, and Paul, the planner asked, "Where are we going to get one of those?"

I said, "We build one. If you guys can help me with getting the materials, I can design it, and together we can build it."

The lack of enthusiasm was a little insulting. I had given this quite a bit of thought, and I was confident that I knew how to do it. My only problem was that I didn't know how to get all of the materials without getting caught. We needed fertilizer, and I was pretty sure that the government could track such a purchase. We needed to have a more surreptitious, untraceable way of getting the fertilizer. We needed blasting caps and dynamite. I knew those were controlled. I also knew we had lots of them in our company. With care we could probably spring one or two sticks and caps loose without being noticed. We needed some electronics, miscellaneous motors, actuators, wire and some mechanical machining.

I laid out my thoughts in more detail. I could see them start to come around. On the third run through the plan, Paul starting jumping in with ideas. I knew then that I had them on board. I was completely confident that with them we could pull this off and not get caught.

Not getting caught took the most energy, thought, planning, and careful execution. Doing a crime is easy. Doing a crime and not getting caught is a lot harder. It takes good planning and nerves of steel to execute.

Most crimes have little planning behind them. They are often committed by people incapable of planning. That is why they are committing the crime. If they were good at planning, they would be working legitimately, probably as a planner.

The police depend on this. They are not equipped to catch perps with planning skills. They have a list of things they look for, and if they don't find them and nobody talks, the crime is never solved. This is a closely held secret. It makes for bad police press.

I had seen Mike and Paul in action. I knew that they were fully capable of pulling this off.

Paul agreed to get the fertilizer, dynamite and caps. Mike offered to drive the chase car, and his guys could help with the electronics. I would to design the system. It would be a lot of fun, and I was looking forward to it. I also agreed to remotely drive the truck with the bomb, but I wasn't so sure that would be fun.

First, I was going to have to contact a guy in my old hometown. He was the only guy who I knew who could do two things for me: machine parts and keep his mouth shut forever. He is The Dragon.

Dragon is a biker. We have ridden together a lot, and I like the guy, but he is not from regular society. He is, well, he is The Dragon.

27
The Dragon

The Dragon was sitting in his garage/shop thinking and smoking. Mostly smoking. He smoked his own roll with whacky weed. It helped even out the rough spots in life. The Dragon figured he had a lot of rough spots. He was thinking this over when his phone rang. Might be business. He could use some business. Yeah, could use some business.

He dug out his phone, remembering in the old days how you had to run to the phone. He successfully got his phone out and answered. It was Jack Clayton. He hadn't seen or heard from Jack in a coon's age. The Dragon heard you aren't supposed to use "coon's age" any more. The Dragon wasn't politically correct. Yeah, not politically correct.

"Hey, Jack how are you doing?"

"Tolerable. How about you?"

"Still here on the right side of grass. I assume you called for more than finding out how I am?"

"Yeah, I need some machining done. I am thinking about dropping by this weekend if you're around."

The Dragon thought about this. There are a lot of places in West Virginia to get machining done. Why come to Ohio? The obvious answer was that Jack was up to something he wanted kept quiet. That was okay with The Dragon. He was a quiet guy. Yeah, a quiet guy.

"Sure, I'll be around. You got a lot of work or what?"

"I have some drawings I made. I thought we could review them Friday afternoon. I think you can do it in one day, but you should take a look and tell me."

"Okay, I'll see you Friday."

The Dragon sat in a cloud of smoke. The good kind of smoke. He took another toke and thought some more. The Dragon knew he could trust Jack, but he still needed to be careful. The machining would be fine and made untraceable, but the materials might be traceable. He probably could use scrap material depending on what Jack wanted done. Scrap wouldn't be traceable.

He didn't have to worry about his neighbors. They knew enough to keep their mouths shut, and if Jack's work was small enough to keep inside the garage, they wouldn't see anything.

The Dragon had a milling machine, an 8-inch swing lathe, a band saw, a power hacksaw, and various other tools. He could do most any machining, plus he had two kinds of welders. Before tackling the job, The Dragon would have to make sure he could do all of the machining. This would be no time to be asking another shop to help. That could raise questions, and it would provide witnesses and possible security leaks. If The Dragon couldn't do all of the machining, he wouldn't do any of it.

He thought the risks would be small, and he was happy to help out a guy like Jack. He had helped Jack build a motorcycle to fit his out-sized body. Gee, he was big. Probably still as big if not bigger. Yeah, if not bigger.

Jack mentioned he might have a woman with him. That was not good. The Dragon didn't like witnesses. Maybe he could talk him out of having her here. But he knew Jack well, and if Jack trusted her, she was all right.

Jack was no dummy.

He worked in finance doing things that The Dragon had no clue on. Big companies have a lot of money to carry around. It must take a lot of people. Jack was big enough to carry a really big pile of money. Yeah, a big pile of money.

Jack was also a scientist. He was always talking about scientific things and explaining how things work. Now he was coming with drawings for a machine of some kind he had designed.

What the heck kind of machine would a CPA want built? And on the QT at that. A wheelbarrow for carrying money? It was enough to make you curious. In this kind of business curiosity can get you killed. Still, The Dragon had a little curiosity. Yeah, a little curiosity.

The Dragon was also curious about a woman who Jack would want hanging around. The last The Dragon knew, Jack wanted nothing to do with women at least for quite a while after his tragic divorce. Maybe he could sic his wife, Nancy, on the woman while she waited for Jack. That would get her out of the shop.

The Dragon was still upset about Jack's divorce. His ex-wife raked him over the coals and forced him to leave town. He wasn't even allowed to see his kids who he loved dearly. Yeah, loved dearly.

What kind of woman would do that to a man? Actually, The Dragon knew the answer to that. It was Jack's ex-wife's grandmother. The grandmother was a Woodward, and she had a load of money. She might even have more money than Jack could carry. She controlled half the state because of her money. His ex-wife's father, who married old lady Woodward's daughter, was a big deal lawyer because of the Woodward money. He could figure all the legal angles, and the old woman could finance it. The Dragon figured that the old lady didn't want Jack to get any of the Woodward money, so she ran him out of town. And people like that looked down on the likes of The Dragon just because he rode a bike and smoked a little weed. Well, actually, he smoked a lot of weed. Yeah, a lot of weed.

Then not only was Jack not allowed to see his kids,

the boy was kidnapped. Jack had asked him to help find the kid. The Dragon did what he could. Jack finally found the boy, but he was dead. That was down in Texas. There was a massacre. A whole slew of people were shot. The guy who the police thought was the ring leader was found with his head turned around backwards. The Dragon knew that Jack was on his son's trail, and he knew that Jack was strong enough to turn a guy's head around. You see that crap on TV and in the movies, but in real life it isn't so easy to break a guy's neck the way that guy's neck was broken. The Dragon had a pretty good idea who did the deed. And it was a good job, too. Yeah, a good job.

The Dragon had never seen that side of Jack. Jack was always on the right side of the law when he lived in town. Maybe Jack had changed. Having your son kidnapped and killed could change a man for sure. Yeah, change a man for sure.

Jesus, The Dragon couldn't even imagine the pain of having a child kidnapped and found dead. You never recover from a thing like that. Its every parent's nightmare. That was why it was so easy for The Dragon to put Jack on the right trail. He put the word out, and everyone he knew worked the grapevine. The Dragon never knew the details, but he knew Jack got a tip by phone as a result of The Dragon putting the word out.

The Dragon took another drag. Good stuff. That reminded him, he needed to be sober Friday, Saturday, and maybe Sunday. Gee, three days in a row. Yeah, three in a row.

28

Woody and Lorraine

Woody hung up his phone. Jack had called. It was good hearing from him. Woody hadn't seen him since his son's funeral. Jack was coming into town on personal business. He didn't say what the business was.

It was a courtesy call to say hi. He had better say hi. He used to live with Woody and Lorraine. If Woody found out that Jack had been in town and didn't stop by, Woody would be terribly offended, and Lorraine would cry.

Jack and Woody had some history together. Jack used to help in the bar when he was going through college. Jack was a bouncer and a super good one. Then there was that night a couple of years ago when Woody got into trouble and asked Jack to bail him out. Things went terribly wrong and Jack got cut up pretty bad. The bad guys paid a dear price for that. Woody made sure they wouldn't walk right again. Bastards.

Woody always wondered if that was part of why

Katherine divorced Jack. The timing was right, but Woody didn't know the details. Woody was blown away when he found out the terms of the divorce. Lawyer bastards were criminals for doing that to Jack. Well, of course it wasn't the lawyers; it was that matriarch, Woodward. She had so much money she could burn it for heat in the winter. With that kind of money you can buy whatever you want.

Jack insisted on taking them out to dinner. Woody recommended a new restaurant in town. It didn't have many tables, but it was excellent. It was a quiet, intimate place. From your table you could view the chef preparing your food. But what made it really special was that you could discuss your meal with the chef and have it prepared the way you wanted—as long as the chef approved. The chef knew what he was doing and made great recommendations. If you wanted something special, you could tell the chef ahead of time, and he would have it ready. It was gourmet food, and it was not cheap, but Woody would arrange a special deal for his friend.

They would have a seven course dinner. Woody would talk with the chef and have it all fixed up. He would arrange for the best table. It would be easy because Woody and Lorraine were part owners of the restaurant. He didn't tell Jack that. Let him be surprised.

Woody and Lorraine knew a chef who had wanted to start a restaurant, but he didn't have enough capital. They knew he was a good chef and decided to jump in. They had the money and wanted to expand their business interests. They also wanted something upscale compared to their bar. The bar made good money for them for many years, but the restaurant was going to be more fun. So far it looked like they would break even in their first year, which is a good deal in the restaurant business. Even better, their business was growing, so next year it looked like they would make a lot of money.

Jack said he was bringing a woman with him. That was a total surprise. He thought Jack was done with women, at least for a while. He said her name was Lydia, and then he remembered that she was with him at his son's funeral. That had been a tough day, and he didn't remember her much. He did remember that she was tall like Jack, and she was quiet.

Woody had insisted that Jack and Lydia stay with them while in town. That brought up the sensitive subject of how many bedrooms would be required. Jack told him that Lydia would need her own bedroom. That meant they weren't living together at least not in the same bedroom anyway. Woody would leave it to Lorraine to get the scoop on their relationship.

Jack could have his old room, and Lydia could take one of his daughters' rooms. The girls were grown and had left home. His daughters now had families of their own. Wow, where had the time gone?

Woody was kind of curious as to what the personal business was. Since it was personal, he couldn't very well ask about it. He couldn't think of any business that Jack would have in town. He had severed his ties when he left. Woody knew he didn't have visitation rights, so it wasn't about that—unless Jack had figured a way around the restrictions. That didn't sound like Jack though. When Jack left, he had decided not to try to see the kids. In fact, after the funeral his ex-father-in-law offered to reopen negotiations on visitation, and Jack turned him down in the interest of the daughter. Jack said it would be too confusing and stressful for the young girl. Woody had a lot of respect for Jack having that much love for the child rather than selfishly insisting on visitations. It was a tough deal. Woody didn't think Jack would be working on that. That left Woody without a clue. Well, it was none of his business anyway. What would be his business was making sure that Jack and Lydia had a great time Friday night at the new restaurant.

Lorraine insisted on having Jack and Lydia at their house for dinner Saturday night. That would be super. They could have a nice quiet evening, and Lorraine was a good cook. Woody would make sure he could take both evenings off. He used to work in his bar every night, but he had found an excellent manager to take over most of the management work. Woody had to do that to free up time and energy to start the restaurant.

He hoped that Lorraine and Lydia hit it off. There

was nothing worse than good friends having wives or significant others that didn't get along. He would find out on the weekend. It was coming up fast. Woody and Lorraine had a lot of work to do to get ready.

29

Trip to Ohio

It was Friday morning, and I made sure Lydia was getting ready so we could leave before 8 o'clock. I wanted to get to The Dragon's place early in the afternoon, and we had to stop at Woody and Lorraine's house before going to The Dragon's shop. What I really wanted to do was drop Lydia off with Lorraine while I went to see The Dragon. I wasn't happy about Lydia being around the shop. The less she knew the better.

And seeing The Dragon might send her into a state of shock. The Dragon wasn't your regular citizen. In fact, he wasn't a citizen. He was a hard core biker. I always got along with bikers even though technically I wasn't one of them. I could talk the talk and walk the walk. I rode with The Dragon and his crew quite often. I missed those days.

I cooked breakfast while Lydia was finishing her packing. Both of us had packed the night before, but there are those last minute items like your toothbrush. I wasn't sure what we would be doing for lunch, so I cooked a big breakfast. I would have my usual six eggs, but I added ham and grits.

Grits is an interesting dish. It is typically a southern dish, but it actually came from Native Americans. It is basically ground maize or corn boiled in water. You can eat it that way, but I like to season it, and butter in mine is a must. And I do mean butter. No margarine for me, thank you.

To this I added toast, fresh squeezed orange juice and coffee. I have a special toaster because I like to bake my own bread, and homemade sliced bread is thicker than store bread. I have a bread slicer that will cut bread thinner, but homemade bread tends to fall apart if sliced too thin. Commercial bakeries put ingredients in their bread to make it like sponge rubber. It holds together, but it also has no taste and little food value.

I put out an assortment of jams for Lydia. I liked just butter on my toast, and I didn't want it melted in the toast. I like to butter the toast just before I eat it with the butter on the surface of the toast. I am sure that is the way God wanted us to eat it. Only heathens melt their butter into the bread like they do in restaurants. To save time, restaurant cooks like to have a pot of melted butter with a brush. They brush the butter on like thin paint or stain. That is no way to eat toast.

There was a bang on the door, and Lydia came in, toting a suitcase. She had on some makeup, which was very unusual. She was beautiful, and I felt that tingle from my head to my toes.

Makeup doesn't necessarily improve on Mother Nature, but if done right, it can highlight natural features. It can make things pop and Lydia was popping.

I had oatmeal ready for her. She likes it with raisins, maple syrup and milk. There is nothing wrong with that. I often have it that way as well. In fact, I was the one who introduced her to it. She had toast and the predictable jam. She was eating carefully so as not to disturb her makeup, which she is not used to. As I watched her eat, I thought maybe I should have had oatmeal, but I tore into my eggs and ham.

We finished up, and I threw the dishes in the

dishwasher while Lydia put the jam and other things away.

We put our suitcases in the Lexus ready to roll when I remembered The Cat. Frankie was going to come over to feed and give him water while we were gone. Mike wouldn't come because The Cat had bitten him a couple of times. Frankie wouldn't be over until night time and The Cat likes his water fresh, so I went back in the house and gave him fresh water. He heard me and came walking out to check out the water. I gave him a pet and checked to see that he had plenty of food.

When doing all of that, I wondered whose cat he was. He was supposed to be Lydia's cat, but I seemed to be the one taking care of him. He bit her a few times and that didn't help the relationship. I think she is a little afraid of him. It didn't used to be that way. He has grown an attitude since living in The Cabin.

I squeezed into the Lexus, and we were on our way. It was only one hundred and fifty miles to our destination. Some of it was mountainous, but most was Interstate and fast. All of it was hilly and beautiful except for where they cut the Interstate through the mountains. A mountain in the way of making a straight, level road? No problem. Dynamite and heavy machinery can fix that. The destruction of Mother Nature's work was both amazing to me and an offense toward Her. I was conflicted. I enjoyed the beautiful road, but I wasn't sure we were treating Mother Nature right.

As we motored on, we passed the spot where the trooper found me on the side of the road vomiting. My size and leather motorcycle jacket scared the heck out of him, and he called for a backup, which turned out to be a woman. I, and I think the woman trooper, got a big kick out of it. I think it might have been a while for the guy to live down having a woman trooper bail him out. Male troopers tend to have strong egos, which isn't consistent with having women helping them.

I was sick from the stress of having recently killed a man and witnessing another one killed and on top of that was voted on by a group of people to see whether they would kill me or not. Color me green. I lost my lunch.

I didn't reminisce out loud. Lydia didn't need to

know every detail of my life. A story like that one is like a sweater. You pull on a thread and the whole thing unravels. You can't just tell part of the story. Why were you stopped? I was sick. Why were you sick? I had just killed a man. Why...

We pulled into Woody and Lorraine's as planned, but then everything happened the opposite of what I wanted. First, Lorraine and Woody insisted that we stay for lunch. I didn't want to spend the time that way. Next, Lydia made it clear she was going with me after lunch. She was smart enough not to say where we were going.

On the edge of being rude, I rushed us out after a nice lunch and drove over to The Dragon's shop. I grabbed the roll of drawings from the backseat and went to the garage door with Lydia tight on my heels. I hesitated at the door. I always had the feeling that there was a fifty percent chance I would be shot when I opened the door. I don't know why. In all the years that I knew The Dragon he hadn't shot me once. I knew he carried a 380 Bodyguard in his pants pocket.

I opened the door. It was pleasantly free of smoke.

That was encouraging. The Dragon was probably on the wagon so he could do the machining. He never smoked or drank when working.

The Dragon got up out of his chair. His eyes were surprisingly clear, a good sign. I introduced Lydia to The Dragon, and they exchanged pleasantries.

We went over the drawings. I explained what I wanted in case the drawings were not clear. He said that he would have to phone around for some of the material, which was not a problem. He pointed out he would be using scrap material, so it wouldn't be possible to trace its purchase. Plus, he would use cash. I took the hint and handed him a roll of bills. After a couple of hours of discussion I was ready to leave.

I wanted to stop and see Ann, my former fiancée, but I didn't know how to do that with Lydia with me. My relationship with Ann was strictly platonic, but try and explain that. Ann and I had become good friends after our romance cooled. My wife, now ex-wife, was always testy about the friendship. No point in testing it with Lydia.

I could hardly wait to get back in the car and hear Lydia's thoughts on The Dragon.

30

Holy Smokes

Lydia had worked on a large campus for years, and she knew the odor of marijuana smoke when she smelled it. The odor of it in The Dragon's shop was so thick it seemed like you could grab a hand full. A drug sniffing dog would run in circles in that building and whine in confusion. Might even pass out.

She thought The Dragon was sober. She saw the refrigerator in the corner, and she was willing to bet a hundred dollars, which she didn't have, that it was full of beer. The clue was a trash can of empties.

The Dragon was a sight to behold. He was not a big man physically, but she got the feeling that he was tough as nails. She noticed that in preparation for the trip Jack always talked about him in respectful tones.

He was dressed in clean jeans and a Tee shirt with a small hole in it. His Tee shirt had a pocket in it. His arms were exposed and she could see his tattoos. He had a dragon tattooed on each arm. She guessed it was one reason why he was called The Dragon although it could be the other way around. The tattoos were colored and were of high quality.

She could see the subtle bulge in his pants. The Dragon was carrying a gun. It was barely noticeable. Most people wouldn't notice it, but someone who is carrying or accustomed to carrying is sensitive to these matters. It is called printing. She had no doubt that he knew how to use it and was probably a good shot.

He was polite to her and his language clean, but she would take a second hundred-dollar-bill bet that it wasn't always the case. His movements were slow and measured. He was a guy who did not waste motion. But according to Jack, The Dragon was fast as lightning when needed.

They started discussing the drawings and ignored her except she noticed The Dragon kept an eye on what she was doing. She sat in a chair and discretely looked around the garage.

The discussion went on and on. She began to think that Jack was right in thinking she should stay with

Lorraine rather than tag along. They talked in detail on each drawing, discussing the dimensions, the materials, the processing, and probably more, but Lydia tuned out.

She might have flipped out, but a woman came in and introduced herself as Nancy, The Dragon's wife. Who knew The Dragon was married? Jack had never mentioned it, and surely, he must have known.

Nancy invited her upstairs for tea. Looking for any kind of relief, she accepted and followed Nancy up a set of long stairs running up the outside of the building. The stairs looked rickety, but they seemed solid when they walked on them.

Nancy was dressed in jeans and a shirt. Hers didn't have any holes in them. They were clean but not fancy. The jeans were tight with no bulges, so it seemed that she wasn't carrying. There might be a gun in a nearby purse though.

At the top of the stairs they went through a door into a cozy little kitchen. They sat at a kitchen table where Nancy served tea. Lydia wondered how many customers were invited to have tea. Her question was partially answered when Nancy spoke.

"I thought you might be going nuts with them guys talking engineering. I know it bores the heck out of me."

"Yes, I was ready for the farm. Thanks for rescuing me. It was kind of you. Do you know Jack well?"

"Not real good. We belong to different parts of society, but we used to ride together. Jack and Dragon used to work on motorcycles together."

"Do you know Woody?"

Nancy started to get suspicious. These were too many questions, too soon. But then she realized this was Jack's girlfriend, and she was trying to get a handle on his background. Nothing wrong with that. She could give Lydia some lowdown.

"Yeah, we know Woody. Bikers hang out in his bar. Jack used to bounce there."

"Do you know anything about a knifing there?"

"You mean, was Jack cut there? Yeah, I know about it. Jack is a stand-up guy. He never reported it."

Nancy gave Lydia the Reader's Digest version of what happened. Lydia soaked it all up. Jack wouldn't talk about it with her. He only mentioned that there was some trouble, and he got cut. The only reason he said that much was that she had seen his scars. The scars were small because of expert stapling, but they were there. She was interested in the details.

"Dragon describes Jack as walking both sides of the street. He can be a citizen or he can be a biker. On either side he isn't faking it. It is the real McCoy. It is like he is bilingual or something. He can talk the language in each society with ease and be a natural."

Lydia found that interesting. She of course knew Jack rode, but she didn't know about his biker background. The Jack she knew was just a normal guy who rode on weekends and nights.

Tit for tat, Nancy had a bunch of questions for Lydia. She wanted to know about Jack's life in West Virginia, and she wanted to know a lot about Lydia. Lydia saw no harm in sharing the general stuff, the stuff you find out if you lived next door. She wanted to find out more about Jack's former life. This was a golden opportunity. But to get you have to give.

Lydia was particularly interested in a woman named Ann who was a doctor. Ann stapled Jack's arm and side. Ann was romantically linked to Jack at one time, so she wanted to know more about her. She found out some but not as much as she wanted. She needed more time, but her phone rang. It was Jack looking for her. He was ready to leave.

She said goodbye to Nancy and thanked her for the tea and conversation.

31
Nancy

Nancy washed the tea cups and put them in the cupboard. They were her best dishes. She wasn't sure why she brought them out. It wasn't to impress anyone. She didn't often have an occasion to use them. Lydia used to be a professor at a big university, and now she was a consultant. It was a good time to use her good dishes. Anyway, it made her feel good.

Nancy was glad it was her day off. She didn't work on Fridays. It gave her a chance to meet the woman with Jack. She hoped the woman turned out to be a good person. Jack deserved a decent woman after what he had been through. Nancy liked Jack. Most women liked him. He was built like a Greek god. He could make a nun swoon. Aside from that he was good people.

Nancy was pleased with what she saw in Lydia. Lydia was smart, just like Jack. She was a mathematician. Nancy didn't know exactly what a mathematician did, but she knew you had to be smart to be one.

It was obvious that Lydia was in love with Jack whether she knew it or not. Every time she mentioned Jack, her face lit up like a bulb. That made Nancy happy. It would make Dragon happy too because it meant that they could trust her. Nancy could see that Lydia would do nothing to harm Jack on purpose, and she was too smart to do it accidentally.

Nancy also saw something else in Lydia. Lydia had had a tough go of it for some reason, and it had given her an inner toughness. There was a streak of steel in Lydia and an independent spirit. She was one who knew her own mind, and she was a person of strength.

The thing that impressed Nancy the most was that Lydia was not a snob. She sat down in her kitchen, completely at ease. Nancy knew that Jack was a vice president of a company, and that Lydia must earn good bucks at what she did. They must have plenty of money. Nancy noticed the Lexus that Jack was driving. It took money to wheel one of those around. Yet from Lydia's demeanor you would not know that they had any money.

Lydia was like regular people. Jack had found a keeper.

32

A Nice Dinner

After wrapping up business with The Dragon, we headed for Woody and Lorraine's. I was looking forward to dinner. Woody said he had a place picked out. He mentioned the name, but it wasn't any place that I had ever heard of. I had been gone from town less than two years, but things can change fast. It was a college town, so there were several good restaurants.

The business with The Dragon went well. I thought that he would do the job, but there was a possibility that he might turn it down. I had no backup, so I was relieved when he said he would do it and thought he could have it done by Sunday.

Paul was getting some of the other needed materials. In addition to that, I needed a model airplane controller, three amplifiers, a variable speed DC motor and two 12-volt linear actuators. I gave Mike the specs for those, and he said he would get the parts on the Internet, using a phony name and credit card so it couldn't be traced.

The parts would be delivered to a post office box in California and reshipped to Kentucky. Mike would have a guy pick them up and drive them up to West Virginia. Plenty of insulation there.

My plan was to use the linear actuators to push the accelerator and the brake pedal. The controller would send out the signals, which would be too weak for the actuators, hence the amplifiers. The controller would send signals to the third amplifier to power the motor belted to a pulley replacing the steering wheel. I made sure that the controller had plenty of channels, so I could wire up the turn signals. I would turn the turn signals on when making a turn. Might as well drive legally.

From auto shops we would get automotive cameras, so I could see where the truck was going. A camera would be aimed at the truck's dash, so I could see the truck speed. Two more cameras would be aimed at the truck mirrors. The controller and monitors would be mounted in the chase vehicle.

It was going to be busy trying to control all of this in the chase vehicle, so I came up with a plan. I would build out of plywood a unit that would slide in place of the passenger seat. Attached to it would be pedals simulating the accelerator pedal and brake pedal. I would mount the steering wheel from the truck on the board along with turn signal switches. The video displays from the cameras would be mounted on the top of the board. I could "drive" the truck while sitting in the chase vehicle. It was going to take some practice and fiddling with the plywood apparatus, but I was confident that I could make it work.

Also, on the plywood would be a safety switch and a denotation switch with protective covers. If the denotation switch was accidentally pushed, nothing would happen unless the safety switch was also turned to the armed position. I didn't want the truck to blow up unexpectedly.

The tricky part was going to be modifying the airplane controller so I could use the sensors on my plywood apparatus as inputs to the controller to be broadcast to the receiver in the truck. Also, the receiver in the truck would have to be wired to the amplifiers and turn signals. I couldn't do it, but Mike had a guy who could. That part made me nervous, but he said he could make it work.

I was personally going to build the plywood assembly at Mike's farm. Mike would help me. I had The Dragon machining the metal parts we would need for that and for the actuator installations in the truck. It was going to be a lot of work. After that it was going to take time to practice driving the truck remotely. It would take us at least couple of weeks after we had all the parts.

Meanwhile it was time to have an evening of fun. Lydia and I took showers and got ready. We went downstairs and Woody made drinks for us. He made old fashioneds with Maker's Mark bourbon. Lorraine stayed with her vodka martinis. I had brought a bottle of vodka for her. If I showed up without it, she would think I didn't love her any more.

It was still early, so we were having several drinks. I was beginning to be a little concerned about one of us driving. I was musing on this when Woody received a phone call. After the call he announced that our car was ready and out front of the house. Woody explained he hired a limo for the evening, so we could drink as much as we wanted.

The limo took us to a restaurant that I had never seen before. It was new. We went in, and Woody showed us to a table. The chef came over right away and introduced himself to Lydia and me. It was clear that he already knew Woody and Lorraine. Through the conversation with the chef it became clear that Woody and Lorraine were partners in the restaurant.

The chef was dressed in white, including a chef's hat. I thought if the food is as good as his outfit, it would be excellent.

Woody had worked with me ahead of time on the food we would order. We were having Beef Wellington with roasted potatoes. I wanted mashed potatoes of course, but I was outvoted. The whole meal was going to be seven courses. We were going to be there a while. It was well that the chairs were comfortable. The chef started us off with wine. I was beginning to see the wisdom of hiring a car.

We had finished the shrimp cocktail and started on the Vichyssoise (potato leak soup) when my greatest nightmare walked in the door. Bill Simpson, his wife and his daughter A.K.A. my ex-wife walked in. The restaurant was very small with just a few tables, so the chances of us not seeing each other was zero.

Woody saw the look on my face and turned to see what was wrong. His face turned red. It was an awkward moment for everyone, and Woody felt the evening he planned was just involved in a train wreck.

Bill escorted his party to a table, which thank God was not next to our table. It was as far away as you could get, but in a small restaurant, it was not far enough.

The women sat down, and Bill came to our table. He said hi to me. I said hi, but didn't stand up for the handshake. I reminded him that he had been introduced to everyone at Will's funeral.

"Jack, it is good to see you. Katherine and Margret say hi."

Sure they did. They are probably cringing just like the rest of us.

"So, Jack, what are you doing in town?"

"Personal business."

This conversation wasn't going anywhere, but Bill seemed like he wanted to talk. Finally, he came out with it. He wanted me to stop by his office on personal business. I couldn't imagine what kind of business, personal or otherwise, that I might have with him. I didn't want to ask in the middle of our dinner, so I agreed to meet him in his home office the next day. Looking back on it, I think all the joy juice we were drinking affected my judgment.

The Simpsons' appearance threatened to put a damper on dinner, but I made a decision. I wasn't going to let them ruin our evening. They had done enough damage to my life, and I was going to live the way I wanted. I was thankful that they didn't have my daughter, Laura, with them. That truly would have wrecked things.

Bill made it back to his table, and we went on with

our dinner. It surpassed anything I could have imagined. It was great. The chef kept plying us with different wines for each course. I was getting happier and happier, and I soon forgot about Bill and his entourage.

Lydia and I took the crème brûlée for dessert. It was excellent. The sugar on top was caramelized but not scorched. I hate it when a novice burns the sugar. I think Woody and Lorraine had the chocolate torte, but I am not sure.

Woody phoned for the limo. We piled in it like a group of drunken teenagers, giggling and laughing. It would have been disgraceful except we were having such a good time. Tomorrow, I was going to The Dragon's shop. I hoped I wasn't too hungover for, this important deal.

33

A Trip Down Hell's Lane

I got up, showered and shaved without cutting myself, a pretty good accomplishment considering what condition my condition was in. Lydia was still in bed but would be up soon. I went downstairs to find that I was the first one to the kitchen.

I drank some orange juice because I knew I needed the moisture. Water seemed too bland. I dug out the coffee and got a pot going. I made a big one because I knew everyone would be dragging until they had a cup, maybe several cups. I was thinking about making some breakfast when Lorraine came in the kitchen. I lived here years ago, so I knew she didn't mind me in the kitchen.

We sipped on our coffees and talked about breakfast. It was late, so we began calling it brunch. We finally decided that I would make cream cheese crepes with bananas. She just happened to have all the ingredients, which would have raised suspicions in a questioning mind.

We had a nice brunch together. Lydia was more cheerful than I expected. Maybe she was faking it. We had a lot of joy juice the night before. We had a leisurely meal, and I was reluctant to leave, but I had to get to The Dragon's shop to see how things were going. It was almost noon by the time I left Woody's. If The Dragon had enough pieces machined, I planned on putting them together. I had a pair of coveralls and gloves in the trunk for the occasion.

I invited Lydia to go with me since she expressed such a desire before leaving home. She had a change of heart and wanted to stay with Lorraine, which was fine with me. I knew Nancy was working today and that meant Lydia would have to hang around the shop if she came with me.

I got to the shop about 12:30 and put on my coveralls. The Dragon had a pot of coffee on, and I took a cup. I looked over the machining, and it looked good. He had a few questions, which I answered. He said he would have it all completed that night or early Sunday morning.

He was working on one of the more difficult and work intensive pieces, the hub that replaced the steering wheel. The center hole that fits on the steering column is broached, and The Dragon didn't have a broach or broaching machine. That is a very specialized machining operation. To get around this, The Dragon had gotten a steering wheel from a junk yard and was cutting the outside away, leaving just the hub. He would machine a pulley piece that would fit over the hub. He thought about heating the pulley and freezing the hub with a shrink fit. That is a high risk operation because if you don't get the pieces pressed together the first time, the temperatures will even out, and the pieces will be stuck where they are with no way to fix it. We talked about it and decided to go with a close fit and put in set screws or possibly weld it. The pulley might not be exactly centered, but it would be a slow speed operation and didn't have to last long, which I didn't mention to The Dragon. Besides, it would be off center by only a few thousands of an inch and really wouldn't be noticeable with a belt drive.

I put on gloves so I wouldn't leave finger prints and started on the assembly. It went smoothly and everything fit. It looked just like my drawing. I took it apart again, so it would fit in the Lexus trunk. It was 2:30, and I was supposed to be at Bill Simpson's at 3:00. I had no cleanup to do because of my coveralls and gloves. I took them off and was ready to go. The Dragon was busy machining the steering wheel hub. Later, he would machine the pulley and put them together. That would finish the job.

I pulled into Bill's driveway at 2:55. I wanted to be exactly on time, but the traffic was lighter than I expected. Bill had a long driveway around back, so maybe if I drove very slowly, I would get there exactly on time.

I noticed his front door as I drove by. It is the only thing I really like about the house. It is a sprawling red brick ranch with a huge lawn. I drove around back where there is a door going directly to his home office. He had a beautiful office in town, but he did some private work in his home office, especially for clients who didn't want the publicity of his other office. Today we were meeting here because it was Saturday.

I parked and walked slowly to his door, wondering what awaited me. I didn't know exactly why I bothered to come. I didn't really have to. There was the curiosity factor, the fact that I liked Bill, and I didn't want to embarrass people by telling him no in front of so many people in the intimate restaurant. And there was the joy juice.

I tapped on his door, and Bill answered right away. He was expecting me. We shook hands because that is the social convention.

I went in. It was the same old office with a huge desk to intimidate clients and a nice sofa in case they passed out from the bill or something. There were a few comfortable chairs. There also was a wet bar in case a client needed oiling.

Bill asked me if I wanted a drink. I figured why not? Probably not much else good was going to happen to me in his office. He gave me my regular old fashioned with a thick orange slice and two cherries. He knew that I liked fruit. He mentioned it was a double, which would save him from making a second trip to the bar. We sat in the comfortable chairs with our drinks.

I said, "I haven't been here or even in town since Will's funeral. Not much has changed."

He began on his agenda, "Well maybe some things have changed. That is what I wanted to talk to you about. A few months ago Mama almost died. At least she thought she was dying."

As I sat there sipping my drink and listening to him, I wondered if she had packed her bags full of money, so she could take it with her. I'm sure she had made arrangements with God for taking it. I'm either a cynic or a realist. I can't tell which.

Bill continued, "After Will's funeral, it came out about one of the cops in charge of finding Will was corrupt and involved in drugs. It created quite a stir. Mama was beside herself, and she launched an investigation with private detectives. She turned up quite a bit of information, information that seems to corroborate the rumors that you had something to do with Will being found."

This caught me by surprise. I had no idea she was doing this. I wondered if Mike knew. I made sure that I maintained a stone face. I couldn't afford to react one way or the other. I didn't think Bill would be up to something bad, but when the rest of your life is at stake, it is no time to be careless.

He went on, "Anyway, she has convinced herself that if it weren't for you, we would not have gotten Will back. After seeing the reports, I tend to agree with her. I have always believed that I knew who twisted that bastard's head around backwards. It was a good job. I wish I could have been there to help."

"Bill, we have gone through this before. You all are letting your imaginations run away from you."

"I haven't called you here to debate the issue. After the investigation, thinking she was dying, and brooding on things, Mama is convinced that she was wrong about you. She wants the terms of the contract changed so that you can see your daughter, Laura."

I was glad I was sitting down. Otherwise the air conditioner breeze might have knocked me over. I would never have thought of this. I thought it through, looking for angles. I didn't think they would be trying to connect me to the killings because they would have no motive to do so. Still, it was a huge change in her attitude toward me.

"What is she planning?"

"She wants to remove the one hundred yard restriction and allow visiting rights."

"Bill, we talked about this right after Will's funeral. I turned down your offer of trying to renegotiate the contract. I now turn down her offer for the same reasons. You cannot change what has happened. For me to visit Laura at this age would only confuse her and cause her more anxiety. I have no idea what she has been told about my leaving. She probably hates me. I have don't know how to repair our relationship at her young age, and at best, I would only be able to see her on weekends. That isn't enough time to rebuild a relationship. It is not right for Laura. I want to wait until she is older."

"I am not surprised at your decision. I remember clearly our talk after Will's funeral. I mentioned this to Mama, but she was adamant that we change the contract and allow you to visit Laura."

"You know, you people toy with me like a cat plays with a mouse. You have money on your side. I will tell you my plan, and you can pass it along to Mama. I have arranged for a copy of the current contract along with a letter of explanation to be delivered to Laura immediately after her sixteenth birthday. If well, I will do this myself. If not well or dead, I have an agreement with a man to open my bank lock box and deliver the package. He is the kind of guy who doesn't take no for an answer, so the package delivery can't be stopped."

Bill's face turned white. He stared at me as if he were seeing me for the first time.

Being a lawyer, he recovered quickly and said, "That will destroy Katherine and will destroy our relationship with Laura. You can't do such a thing."

"All the destroying was done by you people. I am

only holding up a mirror, and I want Laura to know what happened. This will not be stopped. It is all arranged, and I am not changing it. When you talk with Mama, you can remind her that I did not want this. It is you all who have done the work. You reap what you sow."

There didn't seem to be anything else to say, so I got up to leave. Bill got up, but I could see he was shaky, and it seemed if he had aged ten years. I had to collect my machined parts and get out of this town.

34

Return Home and a Confession

Lydia and I left Woody and Lorraine's right after lunch on Sunday. I wanted to leave earlier, but they insisted that we stay for lunch. It was clear that Lydia and Lorraine had hit if off big time. We had plenty of time, so we stayed. After lunch we headed to The Dragon's den.

We found The Dragon is his shop sitting in his chair. Apparently the work was completed, and surprisingly, he was sober. There was no customary cloud of whacky weed smoke over his head.

I knew all the parts except the steering wheel pulley were good because I had assembled them to check and had disassembled them to fit in the trunk. I looked at the steering wheel pulley, and it looked perfect. I noticed that he welded the parts together. I gave him compliments and asked how much money he wanted. He gave me a figure that I thought was low, so I doubled it and paid him in cash. He didn't protest.

We gathered up the parts and carried them to the car. I had installed a piece of canvas and a sheet of plastic from Lowe's in the trunk to make sure no traces of machine oil or metal chips from the parts would remain in the car. After the job was completed I would destroy the canvas and the plastic sheet.

The Dragon reminded me that he washed the parts down and they were clean, meaning he had wiped his fingerprints off. I never touched the parts with my bare hands, and I made sure Lydia didn't touch them. I noticed Woody wore gloves while helping to carry the parts to the car. He said he had also run a file over all the machined surfaces to remove tool marks, so the pieces couldn't be traced. He would destroy the file. I knew he liked to make knives out of old files so that was probably the fate of this file.

Woody called Nancy down to say goodbye. With that we were ready to roll. I was anxious to get on the road and get back home.

We had a relatively short drive before getting on the Interstate. It is beautiful country, and I didn't mind the drive. I found it relaxing except as Yogi Berra would say it was déjà vu all over again.

It wasn't that long ago that Lydia and I took this route going home from Will's funeral. I glanced over at her, and she had a pensive look on her face. She saw me look at her, and she placed her hand on mine, which was on the center console. It made me feel better.

We got onto the Interstate and started making good time although there wasn't a need. We would get home well before 5 P.M., but hurrying is the American way.

Lydia was quiet, and I was focused on the road. I had a feeling that there was something on her mind. No point in asking.

Finally, she said she had something to tell me. She didn't seem upset, so I thought maybe it wouldn't be too bad.

"Jack, I had a great time this weekend. I loved both Nancy and Lorraine. We had good talks."

More silence. I waited. Miles went by.

She started again, "I learned a lot about you."

This didn't worry me. I had told Lydia all about my

past. I even told her about Ann, which as far as I knew was not a requirement. She even had a pretty good idea about how many men I had killed. I knew there was more to come, and apparently it was a duesy because it was taking her a long time to get it out.

"When you told me you loved me, I didn't exactly say I loved you. I hadn't thought about it. I have thought a lot about it this weekend, and I have come to a decision. I love you very much."

There, it is was out. I turned my hand over and held her hand. It was a good feeling. It was nice returning home again.

35

Mike's Farm and Shop

Monday morning I went to Mike's place as arranged. He has a farm out in the sticks. It is hard to get to. The driveway is dirt and long but in fairly good shape because Mike has a bulldozer, and he keeps the driveway honed.

I drove up to the house. Mike had sensors all over the place, so he knew I was on my way long before I appeared. He was outside waiting for me. That was kind of disappointing because I wanted to see Frankie. Seeing her is like seeing a flower right after it has opened up. Maybe she wasn't up yet. Anyway, I would get to see her later. She would come out to say hi even though Mike didn't like her seeing what we were doing.

I lowered my window as Mike approached.

He asked, "You have the stuff?"

"Is the Pope Catholic?"

"Good, bring it up to the shop I have set up in the barn."

I drove up to the barn and Mike opened the big doors. Inside was a truck cordoned off with plastic sheeting. It had strong lights inside the plastic housing. It was a work shop for working on the truck. It would allow us to keep everything quarantined. Later, after all the work was done, we would take the truck to a truck wash and high pressure wash it with emphasis on the undercarriage, so no dirt from his farm would go with the truck. The FBI can track things like that. In fact, we would wash the truck several times, including in New Jersey. You can't be too careful in this business.

Mike was anxious to see the parts. We took them inside. Mike looked the parts over and noticed that someone had taken a file to all the cut edges and removed the tooling marks. Bits and pieces of them might be left over from the explosion and be traceable, and if the mission failed, then the whole truck and the equipment in it would be available to investigators. The chances of their getting to The Dragon's shop were slim, but why take the risk?

Mike had all the tools we would need in the shop. We

weren't allowed to bring in tools or take tools out without his permission. After the job everything in the plastic workshop, including all the tools, would be destroyed, so they couldn't be traced.

We got busy and drilled holes in the truck floor to fasten the mechanism for operating the pedals and steering wheel. All the drill chips were collected on a plastic sheet under the truck. We took the steering wheel off and began the installation. Paul showed up with a load of parts, including the motors and actuators.

Lunch was in the house, so I got to see Frankie. That gave me my Frankie fix for the day. I gave her a big hug. Mike had gotten used to my hugging Frankie, and he ignored it.

In the afternoon we assembled all the parts I had The Dragon machine in Ohio. It went together well and by five o'clock we had the truck all set to be driven remotely.

We needed to build a rack in the back to hold the barrels of fertilizer at the top of the cab. I wanted the explosion to be directed at the house and not have the cab stop any of the force. We were also going to build a box between the barrels and the front of the truck box filled with steel to act as shrapnel. Paul had collected untraceable ball bearings and other scrap for that.

It was then that Paul delivered the bad news. The fertilizer was way behind schedule. In fact, so far behind that it wasn't going to be possible to get it to the farm in time to keep on schedule. Paul said he was sure he could get the fertilizer to the warehouse in New Jersey where we were going to do the final truck preparation. He thought we could mix the diesel fuel and fertilizer there and load the barrels.

I was shocked. This was not up to Paul's usual standards. We needed a fork lift to lift the barrels in place, and we weren't going to have one in New Jersey. He thought maybe Mike and I could roll the barrels up a plank. I wasn't sure we could do that, plus it was risky. One of us could get hurt.

Then I had an idea. I thought we could use hydraulic jacks to lift the barrels in place. We could build a platform for the barrels and put the jacks under the platform. We talked about this. As with all ideas, it wasn't as simple as first thought, but in an hour or so we had worked out the details. It was agreed that we needed to get the jacks, build the platform, and practice. It was late, and we would start on it the next day. Paul said he would get the jacks.

The rest of the week went better and by Friday we had the truck ready and had practiced with the jacks, using sand in the barrels to simulate the weight. We were going to have to be careful with the sand. It could be traced by the FBI. We had the sand in strong plastic bags, but some might leak out. We would catch most of the sand on plastic sheets, but we would be spending a good deal of the following week cleaning the truck and barrels, getting rid of any wayward sand.

Our next big project was building the chase vehicle. Paul had secured a vehicle. Its modifications would be reversible, and it would be returning to West Virginia after the job. It was a nondescript vehicle, and we would use stolen New Jersey plates when in New Jersey, so it couldn't be traced.

Paul had gotten the model airplane controller and other parts I needed. Mike's guy modified the controller to take the inputs from the sensors we were going to install in the chase vehicle. That would take a couple of days, and then it would be practice time.

We had been working long hours, and I was ready for a break. I planned on taking Lydia to Charleston to see a man about another project I had in mind.

36

Charleston

I convinced Lydia we should go to Charleston for the weekend. It was the nearest "big" city with only about 51,000 population. It is the biggest city in West Virginia and the capital. She didn't know it, but I had found a jeweler who could make something for me. Plus, I had a friend there who would be shopping for a ring for his fiancée.

Charleston is an easy ride up the Interstate from The Cabin. We left right after lunch and would be there by three P.M. I told Lydia we would be meeting my friend, Andy, and his girlfriend, Betty, at a jeweler's shop where they would be picking out a ring. She didn't like it because she said we would be intruding in a personal moment. Yeah, I guess, but it was my only plan. I told her that he had requested that we be there, and besides we were having dinner with them later. Small lies make the world go round. It isn't just money. It's small lies and money that make the world work.

We found our way to the jeweler's store. It wasn't hard because Charleston is so small. I found a place to park, and we walked to the store. I made sure that the jeweler pretended that he had never met me. I didn't want Lydia to know I had been there before.

I introduced us to the jeweler, and reminded him we were to meet friends. We waited and in a few minutes Andy and Betty walked in the store. He was a guy who I knew in college. We weren't that close, but he had agreed to a dinner and a trip to the jeweler's. The trip to the store was a small price to pay for the great dinner we were going to have.

We chatted a little, and then they started their ring discussion with the jeweler who brought out pictures and samples of stones and rings. He sized Betty's finger. While at it he joked around and measured Lydia's ring finger.

They talked about stones. The jeweler casualty involved Lydia in the discussion and found out what kind of stones Lydia liked and the sizes that seemed right. He did a great job. My friend and his girl finally decided upon a ring, and we left the store. They were going home to change, and we were checking into a hotel.

I booked rooms in the best hotel I could find downtown. I booked four rooms, two for the women, one for my friend and one for me. I made sure that there was a joining door between Lydia's room and mine. Having rooms downtown would allow us to take a taxi to dinner and return to the hotel without worrying about driving after having drinks. And, we were going to have drinks.

Lydia and I settled in and got ready for dinner. Our friends showed up, and I called a cab. It was a short drive to the restaurant. The restaurant was higher quality than the hotel. I arranged for a private area in the restaurant, so we could have a quiet time together.

The restaurant served American food with prices so high that I was surprised that they put them on the menu. If you were concerned about the price, you couldn't afford to eat there. My friend had a worried look on his face. I reminded him that it was my treat and that anything on the menu was fair game.

We ordered drinks, appetizers, soup, salad and an entrée. I ordered steak Diane, which came with mashed potatoes. I added a side of white asparagus. Lydia ordered a filet mignon, which also came with mashed potatoes, and she added white asparagus. My friends ordered New York Strip steaks with a horseradish sauce on top. I have had that, and it is wonderful. We ordered four plates of mixed appetizers to share. I ordered a bottle of Malbec red from Argentina and a bottle of Riesling wine from Germany. We were off to a good time. Lydia and I would drink the white wine. I know you aren't supposed to drink white wine with red meat, but we are often reckless with social convention. It is a wonder that we weren't wearing purple.

After dinner we all had Bananas Foster. That is a little risky because sometimes the bananas can be mushy, which isn't good. However, they did a good job, and it was excellent. Since we weren't driving, we topped it all off with a brandy. The brandy was not as good as Bob's, but it was good. The challenge would be walking. It was one of the best dinners I had had in a long time.

I had the restaurant call a cab for us. I wasn't sure if I could work a phone. It is hard for me to use a phone with my big fingers on small buttons, plus we had a lot of laugh juice. I assume it was laugh juice because we were laughing a lot.

We got back to the hotel in good shape and said goodnight to my friends. Lydia and I went to our rooms. She followed me into my room, a sure sign something was on her mind.

She asked, "Jack, how much are the dinner and hotel rooms costing?"

"Why?"

"I just want to know."

"I don't want to tell you, but I can say the tip alone at the restaurant is more than most people spend on several good dinners."

"Why do you do things like this?"

"Because I enjoy it. As far as is known for sure, we live only once, and we might as well make the best of it."

"It bothers me that we spend money like this and other people don't have enough to eat."

I took note that "we" were spending the money, not I.

"I agree, but there is no way that I can fix that. Meanwhile, I am going to enjoy the fruits of my labors, and I greatly enjoy having friends around, especially you."

37

Lydia on the Way Home

The breakfast in their hotel room cured Lydia's small hangover. She lost track of how much she drank, but it was too much. She wasn't sure about an afterlife, but she knew for sure sinners paid for their sins on this earth. She thought it worthwhile because she had a terrific time the night before.

They were on the Interstate and would be home soon. It wasn't very far between Charleston and home, and the Interstate was fast. Jack liked the Interstate way of going, and she guessed it was probably the smart thing to do. When she commuted to Pittsburgh, she often took secondary roads. She liked the scenery and the curved mountain roads. The Interstates were too antiseptic. It was amazing to her what dynamite and huge earth moving machinery could do. Alfred Nobel unleashed a monster.

He created explosives for war, and then felt so guilty that he created the Nobel Prize, a form of apology. At the same time he saved many lives by developing dynamite to replace nitroglycerin. Nitroglycerin was needed to blast through hard rock, but it was very unstable. It tended to blow up at unwanted times. A lot of Chinese were killed that way building the railroad tunnels in the West. That was okay with the white-man because you could get more Chinese, but it caused delays, and time is money. Americans and the Canadians should be ashamed of how the Chinese immigrants were treated. Sadly, most people know nothing of what happened. Dynamite solved the hard rock problem and made blowing up things relatively safe. Tons of it were used to cut through the West Virginia mountains to make straight, level roads. She knew all this nerd stuff because Jack told her, and she found it interesting.

She still had mixed feelings on his restaurant splurges. She had shut off a restaurant trip to New York City because of the money, but he had worked in a big dinner in Ohio and now this trip to Charleston. She thought it wasteful, and she felt bad thinking about all the people without enough to eat. At the same time she agreed with Jack that there was little that they could do about it although she noted that Jack did a lot to help provide jobs for people at The Cabin. He helped Marty and Louise with jobs and the truck garden. Before Jack helped them, they were destitute.

In truth, she was enjoying the meals in expensive restaurants. It was a view on the world that she never had seen before. Jack had introduced her to unbelievable foods. They were scrumptious but fattening. She was going to have to run it off.

The last two weekends were amazing. The dinners were great, and best of all, she had learned tons about Jack. To hear him talk in The Cabin one would think he had no friends, but she found he had several good friends. In fact, people liked him very much. The only people who didn't like him was the Woodward-Simpson clan, and they were a group of snobs.

She learned a lot of factual information from Lorraine and Nancy, but she learned something different at the dinners. She knew Jack was well educated. He read voraciously and could talk on about any subject.

But at the dinners she learned what a sense of humor he has. She knew he had a sense of humor but not the extent of it. He kept them in stitches at dinner. It all had caught her by surprise, and she was seeing more and more how much she loved him.

She reached over and put her hand on his hand on the console. It sent a bolt of electricity through her body when she touched his hand, and it made her feel good to hold his hand. His hands were huge. She was going to have to figure what she wanted with him. Their relationship was getting deeper and deeper.

It amused her. She remembered a year and a half ago how angry she was when he moved into The Cabin. She so much wanted him gone. She felt her territory had been invaded. She said some terrible things to him, but he only treated her kindly. It made her ashamed to think of it.

She guessed that The Cat figured it out first. He liked Jack right from the start. It took her a year and a half but in the end she fell in love with him.

She was worried about Jack. First, he was anxious

because of the way Bob was treating him. Now he was under stress because he was ultimately accountable for the success of the business, and most of all this project in New Jersey was affecting him. Most people wouldn't notice it, but she could sense his tension. Except for these wild dinners, he wasn't eating as much. And the wild dinners. Jack liked good meals, but these last two dinners were off the charts. It was like he knew he wasn't going to live long, and he wanted to make the most of his remaining time. It worried her a lot.

It was funny that she never remembered him talking about Andy until just before the trip to Charleston. She never thought he kept secrets except those that could send him to prison. This Andy popping up was suspicious. And that bit in the jewelry store, what was that all about? It seemed contrived.

You don't go to a store to help your friend buy his girlfriend a ring, do you? True, both Andy and Betty had been married before, so the ring buying wasn't perhaps as sacred as the first time, but still, you don't invite your friend, do you? It seemed like Jack was up to something, but it wasn't clear exactly what it was. She would get to the bottom of it sometime. Right now she was too worried about Jack to think about it.

She didn't like the rings so much, but some of the stones were beautiful. If she and Jack were to buy a ring, it would be a good place to do so, but they were not ready for that step. She wasn't sure she would ever be ready for that.

As they pulled into The Cabin parking lot, she shifted her thoughts to The Cat. She wondered if he would attack her when she went in. Sometimes, if they were away long enough and he didn't get fresh water when he wanted, it made him mad. What a cat. What a life.

38

The Sheriff Doesn't Shoot His Mouth or Toe Off

I was sitting in my apartment thinking things over. I felt good about having a lock on avenging Danny's death. The sabotaging was halted, at least temporarily. The project was back on schedule, and we needed to keep it that way. Things were looking good, but I was going to feel a whole lot better after we dealt with Danny's killers.

I was also happy about our trip to Charleston. The cover was pretty thin, so I wasn't sure Lydia was fooled. She is too smart to fool much, but I was counting on the fact that she wasn't thinking along the same lines as I. At any rate I had phoned the jeweler and gave him instructions on what to do.

I was worried though. We had spent all of our efforts on Danny's avenging and stopping the sabotaging. I was okay with the priority, but we had to keep in mind Bob's shooting. Mike was working on it by shaking the bushes about the old days. He hadn't come up with anything. I couldn't tell if it was because there was nothing there or if it was because we weren't spending enough effort on it.

In the mean time we had Bob guarded day and night and The Cabin fortified. It was costing us a lot of money, but we had no choice. As soon as the New Jersey thing was over, we would turn our full attention to Bob's shooter.

The cops' rule of thumb is if the murder or shooting isn't solved in the first forty-eight hours, then the chances of its being solved are very low. Well, we weren't the cops. We would run down every angle until it was solved.

I had spent part of the morning talking with Bob in the library. The Cat followed me to the library. He likes to hang around me. I had to give Bob updates. He was well enough to get around The Cabin a little bit, but he wasn't strong enough to handle business. I tried to keep the worry stuff away from him, but he insisted on knowing what was going on. I briefed him on our New Jersey plan. Much to my relief he agreed with it. We were set to go next Wednesday. We still had a lot of work to do, but it was doable. Just then my phone rang.

It was the sheriff. He wanted to use our range for shooting, and he was alone. We usually didn't let people shoot on the range alone. I sometimes let Danny shoot alone, but I didn't like it. It was safer if there were two people there as long as both of them were responsible and knowledgeable shooters. The sheriff wanted to know if I would shoot with him for an hour or so. I hadn't been to the range for quite a while with everything that had been going on, so I told him yes. He would be there in twenty minutes.

I got out my 9 mm handgun and a box of ammunition. I grabbed my ear protection and was ready to go when the sheriff rolled up.

He eased out of his car, and I hardly recognized him. He had lost a lot of weight. I wanted to ask why and how he lost the weight, but you can't really do that. It could be an illness or some reason that was private. I made a note to listen for clues.

I also made a note to listen to any information he had

on his efforts in finding Bob's shooter. Most people were skeptical that the sheriff would turn up anything. I wasn't so sure. He seemed pretty sharp to me. He had an easy mountain way about him, and he talked slowly, but I detected a native intelligence that should not be underestimated. My plan was to see what he knew without asking much. Cops don't like it if you question them. Asking questions is their job.

We exchanged pleasantries and headed for the range. It was a short walk. I was carrying my 9 mm and a box of ammo. He was carrying just a box of ammo. He was going to shoot his 9 mm Glock, which was mounted on his belt.

Glocks are the favorite of police. Glocks have no mechanical safety. I prefer a mechanical safety. Behind this is a divide in the handgun world. There are mechanical safety adherents and there are those who do not believe in mechanical safeties. There is no in between. You are in one camp or the other. The sheriff like most cops was a no-mechanical-safety guy. The consequence of this was that sometimes cops shoot their toes or feet when holstering their Glock. If the trigger is caught on the holster, the trigger can be pulled as the handgun is inserted in the holster followed by a bang and ouch.

The reason cops like guns without safeties is because when they draw their weapon, there is a good chance that someone is either shooting at them or is about to. Under those conditions it is no time to be asking yourself if you clicked the safety off. Instead you want to be shooting. It could mean your life.

I was never in that situation. In fact, if I drew my weapon to shoot someone, I wanted to take plenty of time to make sure I really wanted to do it. If I got killed in the process, so be it. The chances of my being in that situation were some place between nil and zero. I was more conservative, and I believed in mechanical safeties, at least for me. I also believed in safeties for Lydia, which is why I encouraged her to retire her .32 Kel-Tec. I bought her a Beretta Tomcat. It is a little small for her hand, but it fits in a purse or pocket nicely. It has a mechanical safety. It is also a tip-up gun, so you don't have to rack it. It is too small to hold for racking.

Once on the firing line, there wouldn't be much talking with the gunfire and ear protection, so I gently prodded him for an update on finding Bob's shooter as we walked.

He didn't talk much, but I gathered that he had no new facts. He had some kind of theory that he didn't want to talk about. He seemed to think he knew who the shooter was, but couldn't prove it. That was interesting information but not new. Most people thought the sheriff was deluding himself.

I took the opportunity to encourage the sheriff to keep after it. He seemed pleased that someone thought he was capable of solving the crime. I figured why not encourage him. It didn't cost me anything, and who knows maybe he will do it. If he doesn't, at least we would have this one avenue run down.

As for the weight, the sheriff was anxious to tell me all about it. He was proud of his accomplishment. He said he was tired of carrying his belly around and decided to change his life style. I congratulated him for his tough decision and the stamina to carry it out.

The sheriff was a damn good shot. He beat me hands down. He shoots more than I do. I am a good shot but not a great shot. The sheriff is a great shot.

I think his size helps him shoot. He is a very big man. He isn't as tall as I am, but he weighs more. My weight is mostly bones and muscle. His is largely fat, which was going away. I like the sheriff, and I admire his strength to change his life style so drastically.

We wrapped up. The sheriff left, and I went back in the The Cabin. As I went in my apartment, The Cat gave me a menacing look, so I gave him a fresh bowl of water.

I had to get back to work on the chase vehicle.

39

The Chase Vehicle

The chase vehicle was the vehicle that Mike and I would ride in following the truck with the explosives. I would be busy driving the truck remotely and watching the monitors.

Mike's electronics guy had wired up all the sensors to the model airplane controller. He had also wired up the receiver in the truck to the brake, accelerator and steering motor. He had checked it out and had it working. The next step was for me to practice. I thought the more practice, the better, and we didn't have many days left before the vehicles had to be taken to New Jersey.

The guys had gotten a black Chevy SUV for a chase vehicle. I don't like Chevy's, but that is the way the cookie crumbled. I was going to sit in the back seat. They had taken out the front passenger seat to make room for my plywood box with the mock-up of the inside of the truck with a steering wheel, accelerator, brake, turn signal switches, and several monitors. They had it all set up and checked out for functionality.

I got in and tried it out. They had done a good job in sizing it, but we needed to move it forward some to accommodate my long legs. Everything worked fine except the steering wheel. They had return springs on the brake and accelerator pedals to give a simulated tactile feel. They were unable to figure out a good way of providing tactile feel on the steering wheel. We added a dash-pot and springs, which helped, but it wasn't the same as the real thing. It was clear to me that I was going to have to practice the steering a lot to get used to the feel.

We marked out a course in an open field on Mike's farm with flags. I practiced driving the vehicle through the course. It was tough, but as the hours slipped by I got more skilled. It was difficult watching only the monitors. The natural reaction is to look out the window at the truck. That wouldn't work. I had to keep my eyes on my monitors in the chase vehicle.

Some of the time Mike drove the chase vehicle

behind the truck and sometimes he parked it. The field wasn't large, and I could control the truck from a sitting chase vehicle. There was no point in Mike practicing driving the chase vehicle. It drove like a standard Chevy SUV.

I drove the truck around the field by remote control with the chase vehicle parked. As the truck passed us the first time Mike burst into laughter. I was watching the monitors, and Mike was watching the truck. When it went by with no driver, he said it was the funniest thing he had ever seen. We had been so focused on making the system work that we hadn't given much thought to what the truck would look like. It was clear we needed a mannequin or some sort of dummy sitting in the truck driver's seat posing as the driver. Otherwise, some helpful citizen was liable to phone the cops about the truck on the road with no driver. We phoned Paul, and he got right on finding a mannequin, a wig and a hat. Mike wanted to name the dummy. I didn't think we should get that attached because he was going to heaven in a flash of fire with or without me. I hoped it was without me for the time being. Hoyt Axton, RIP.

We adjusted the camera orientations half a dozen times, trying to get the right angles. I remember taking driver education, and they taught students to line up a part of the car hood with the side of the road to center the vehicle in the lane. I had to do a similar thing, but the cameras had to be at the right angle.

I practiced driving in straight lines and turning corners. Turning corners was a little tricky, and I put the rear wheels in a ditch more than once. One time we had to use Mike's farm tractor to pull the truck out. In all cases we had to back the truck up, and that was tricky because the truck had no steering wheel. I had to hold the brakes on the truck, and another person had to go in the truck and shift into reverse. Then I had to back the truck out with no backup camera although we had cameras pointed at the mirrors, which helped. We talked about putting on a backup camera but we were out of channels on the controller. The bomb run had to be done perfectly with no backups. I was going to have to keep the truck out of the ditches on the bomb run.

Turning into the driveway was going to be tricky. There was a ditch there that I could get the back wheels in if I wasn't careful. We practiced turning that corner endlessly.

One of our concerns was if the bomb didn't detonate, the truck would be stuck facing the bad guy's house with no way of getting it out of there. That would leave the truck, the explosives and all of the electronic and electrical equipment there for the authorities to investigate. We had taken precautions to make sure none of the equipment was traceable, and the truck was going to be cleaned to make sure that there was no DNA or traceable material in it or on it. We would have to use hazmat suits to load the explosives in the warehouse.

To help ensure detonation, we set off several caps with the system. It worked fine. It seemed like we had done everything possible to prevent failure and had a plan in case of failure.

Lydia came out to watch. I wasn't too crazy about her seeing the operations, but then she knew almost everything about it. The only thing she didn't know were the names of some of the players. In fact, I didn't know some of the names. She was curious about all the controls and rode in the chase vehicle next to me. By that time I was keeping the truck out of the ditches.

After a few days of practice, I felt ready for the road. Mike was noticeably nervous, which I found interesting. He was the guy who had gone on many high risk missions in the military. He had also played a major role in getting my son back. I didn't see him in the military, but on the mission to Texas to get my son he was cool as a cucumber. His nervousness was unsettling to me. It made me think he thought I couldn't handle it.

In any case I pushed for an on-road test. We mapped out a route without much traffic, and it was a complete circuit with no backups.

Off we went. We kept the speed low, mostly below twenty miles per hour. It was scary, but I think I did much better than Mike anticipated. We made it round the loop with no incidents, but our speed was too low. We made two more loops and knocked off for the day.

The next day Paul wanted to talk. He had been in

contact with Snake the night before. They thought we were too rushed, and they wanted to push the main event back a week. Paul felt we needed the time and there was nothing sacred about next Wednesday.

Also there was the question of getting the vehicles to New Jersey. We had tentatively planned on Mike and me driving them down, but that was going to take a whole day. We needed alibis and driving would give us no alibis. We were hoping that the bombing would be blamed on a rival biker gang, but we couldn't count on that. If the investigation went wider, Mike and I would be prime suspects. We needed alibis.

Mike and Paul proposed that we let Snake and his helper drive the vehicles to New Jersey. They wouldn't be suspects and didn't need alibis. We could fly both of them from New Jersey in the company plane, so there would be no records. This also jibed better with the fertilizer operations as well because as a matter of fact we still didn't have the fertilizer. The fertilizer snafu was beginning to worry me.

Paul proposed that Mike and I fly down on the

company plane the afternoon of the blast, leaving our credit cards with him. He would fill up Mike's car at a self-service gas station using Mike's credit card and buy groceries at a self-service checkout using my credit card. This would make it look like Mike and I were in West Virginia that evening at the time of the blast, and there would be no witnesses when using the credit cards. There probably would be cameras in the self-service gas station so Paul would wear some of Mike's clothing and be hunched over to look shorter like Mike.

I agreed with the plan. It gave us more time and decreased our risks. It irritated me because on principle I hate to change schedules. So did Paul, which is an additional reason why I agreed so readily. I figured if Paul thought it well to change the schedule, we ought to do it. Plus, secretly this gave me time to do something else that no one knew about. It gave me time to go to Charleston to pick up two items. So I made my trip to Charleston. I thought the items were beautiful.

40

Fertilizer

I could see that even Paul was getting nervous about the lack of fertilizer. Privately, I thought the real reason for the schedule change was due to the problems in getting the fertilizer. We had a grand plan of getting the fertilizer from various places in the U.S. in small quantities in each place. This did two things for us. First, the loss of small quantities tend to fall under the radar. They are usually written off by a store as "shrinkage" and not reported.

Second, it made it hard for the authorities to track it. If they had tracers in the fertilizer, they would get markers from all over the U.S., which wouldn't give them much to go on. We weren't sure if there were markers and didn't want to leave a trail trying to find out.

One thing we were sure of was that dynamite did have markers, so my plan of getting the dynamite from our work site was nixed. Snake got two sticks of dynamite from a southwest source along with blasting caps.

Using fertilizer and diesel fuel as an explosive is interesting. It seems too mundane to be an effective explosive and yet is it used everyday in certain industries. In fact, about 80% of all industrial explosions in the U.S. are done with ANFO (ammonium nitrate and fuel oil). In limestone quarries they routinely drill six-inch holes twenty feet deep in a line. When the holes are ready, they come along with a tanker full of ANFO and pump the holes full. The mixture is very stable, meaning it doesn't blow up easily. It needs a shock wave to set it off. Therefore a primary explosive like dynamite is required to set it off. They will set off a whole line of holes filled with the mixture and blast off a wall. They use front end loaders and huge dump trucks to haul the pieces to a rock crusher to make concrete aggregate and crushed rock for other applications. It is all routine.

After weeks of sweating it out and delays, the fertilizer finally showed up in the warehouse in New Jersey. Snake and his associate had the fertilizer and diesel fuel ready to mix. They would mix the fertilizer and diesel fuel the day before driving the vehicles to New Jersey.

They would mix the materials in a plastic sheet lined box they built. ANFO is hygroscopic, so it would be put in plastic bags to keep most of the moisture away from it. The barrels would be on the platform on the truck bed. When ready, we would load the plastic bags into the barrels. When the barrels were filled, we would jack the platform into place and block it up. We would remove the jacks because they could be salvaged. There was no point in blowing them up.

Mike and I were flying down late the day of the event. We would go to the warehouse and help finish the preparations. Mike and I were the ones who had practiced jacking the platform, with the barrels on it, into place in the truck. That had to be done just right to prevent the platform from wedging on the sides.

As the time for the big event neared, I became nervous. I don't know if the other guys were nervous or not. Mike seemed to have calmed down since everything was in place. Lydia hovered around me. I don't know if she was trying to calm me or herself. We had put a lot of work in this operation and everything rode on a smooth execution.

In particular it depended on me driving the bomb truck from the warehouse to the biker house, a distance of about five miles. It was going to be the longest five mile drive of my life. Mike would try to time it to keep us out of traffic, but I had to keep the truck on the road and on the right side of the road. My biggest worry was making the right angle turn into the driveway. I couldn't swing too wide, but if I got too close on the inside of the turn the back wheels could drop into a ditch. I had demonstrated several times in practice how I could easily do this. We would have no way of backing the truck up, and it would be game over although we could blow the truck up so the authorities wouldn't have as much evidence to go on.

I kept going over it in my head, but that wasn't helping. I would be better off forgetting about it until it was time to drive. I knew that I was going to be sweating heavily, so I made a note to bring a change of clothes. The day was fast approaching. I was starting to sweat already.

41

Ready to Roll—Oops

Finally, it was time to put the final operations in motion. I had the company plane fly Snake and his assistant to West Virginia. They were staying overnight at Mike's place.

We had a meeting to go over the last minute details and to make sure everything was ready. Snake told us how they had prepared the ANFO and had it ready. The warehouse bays were ready for them to back the vehicles in.

Paul had his checklist. It was a long and detailed list, including such minutia as Mike and I giving him our credit cards. Nothing was left to chance or memory. We each were given our own detailed checklist to take with us with instructions on how to destroy it when we were done with it.

After the meeting we took the actuators off the truck and replaced the steering wheel for the trip to New Jersey. Mike and I would replace the actuators in New

Jersey. We packed the tools to do that. After we reset up the truck with actuators, we would run a complete check to make sure everything was working.

Snake and his helper would start off early the next morning. It would take them about eight hours to drive there. Mike and I would fly out in the afternoon on the company plane. We were all set.

I went back to The Cabin. I needed to calm my nerves by cooking. I wanted to make lasagna. I didn't often make lasagna. It is easy to make, but usually it is a large dish. Then I thought why not make a very large dish and invite Frankie, Mike, Snake and his assistant over for dinner along with Lydia? I gave Frankie a call and set it up, so she wouldn't cook dinner.

We had a nice time. I served both red and white wines although Snake and his assistant drank beer with dinner. Heathens. I like a beer once in a while but not with dinner. They left about nine. Snake and his assistant were leaving early the next morning.

I slept some, but was restless. I got up early and went for a run. Snake and his cohort were well on their way.

Back at The Cabin I showered and shaved and was ready for breakfast when Lydia came in. We had oatmeal, toast, juice and coffee.

We were just finishing when the alarm went off that a car was entering the parking lot. I glanced up at the monitor and saw that the car was coming fast. It was Frankie. She came bursting in my apartment the most upset that I had ever seen her.

Breathless, she told us Mike was in the hospital. He just had his appendix taken out on an emergency basis. He was okay, but there was no way he could go to New Jersey for the next few days.

I thought things over. The ANFO was already mixed and in the warehouse. Snake and his cohort would be arriving at the warehouse later in the day, expecting Mike and me to show up. They had the dynamite and caps. It was too late to postpone the event. Lydia and Frankie were looking at me.

I said, "It is too late to postpone. I have to go ahead."

I didn't want to use Snake as a driver because we needed him as a spotter. I didn't know his cohort. In fact, I didn't even know his full name. It was risky to use him, but what other choice did I have?

Lydia was way ahead of me, and she about floored me when she said, "I'll drive."

I was aghast. I couldn't let her drive. Bob would kill me.

I said, "No. I can't let you do that."

"It isn't your choice. It's mine. I know how to drive. I watched you for the better part of a week. I rode in the chase vehicle. I can do the job. I want to do the job. You have no other viable choice."

My mind was in a whirl. First, Mike was in the hospital, and now Lydia wanted to drive. Worse, I thought she was right. So I said, "Okay."

The moment I said it I knew there would be hell to pay. This was directly involving her in a crime, a deadly crime. We were going to rob three people of their lives.

I knew Bob would skin me alive. Bob treated Lydia like a daughter. He was expecting me to act responsibly, and he wouldn't view this as being responsible. I decided to retract my okay.

I said, "No, Bob would kill me. You don't even know the route. I can't let you do it. There must be some other way."

Frankie stepped in and offered to drive. That was no better. Frankie hadn't been in the chase vehicle and knew a lot less than Lydia.

Lydia was agitated and said, "Look, this isn't your decision or Bob's. Bob needs to realize that I have grown up. It is my decision. Danny was as much a friend to me as he was to you guys. I need to do it for him. As far as the route goes, you can make a map, and I can study it on the plane. I have a good memory. I'll memorize the route, every detail. We can make it work."

I looked into her eyes, and I saw a defiance that I had not seen before. It dawned on me how important this was to Lydia. Bob was going to have to live with it. Lydia was the chase driver.

I told Frankie that no one other than Mike and Paul could know about this. It had to be a secret until after the deed was done. She agreed and we started making preparations for the trip. Lydia gave Frankie a credit card to give to Paul for the alibi.

There was just one other major thing I had to do before the trip. After Frankie left, I asked Lydia to accompany me to The Rock.

42

Rocks in My Pocket

Lydia was a little puzzled about my request to go to The Rock. She reminded me that we had to get ready to go to the plane. I reminded her there was no packing, and we were ready to go. She demurred, and we started down the path.

It was a nice summer day, and I took note of all the life around me. There were huge trees, hundreds of years old. Moss was growing on the sides of some of the trees. There were squirrels on limbs above our heads chattering away. Probably didn't want us in the woods. The path was soft from all the dead leaves trying to go back to soil. The sky was blue with a few clouds, but we wouldn't see it until we emerged from the woods.

It was relaxing to me, and I took Lydia's hand. Who knew what lay before us? Perhaps this would be our last day on earth. No one knows the future. We plan and act like we know, but we don't. The only thing we have for sure is the present, and it is fleeting. The best advice comes from Buddhists who advise us to be present in the present.

I chatted with Lydia, telling her how amazing the last year and a half had been. On this point she agreed whole heartedly. She had changed from a recluse to a charming woman. She was a woman of high intelligence and character. I came to the mountains, an injured man who needed to find a job to survive. I now made more money than I could spend. I was investing and rapidly building an estate.

During the bomb planning phase, I made a personal plan. I set up my estate so that if anything bad happened to me, my assets would go to Lydia. She didn't know this and didn't need to know.

We emerged from the woods into the field where The Rock is. Here there wasn't as much of a path, just a small trail through the high grass. The grass was dry and golden. Now we could see the sky. The golden grass contrasted with the blue sky was beautiful.

We were fast approaching The Rock, and I was getting nervous. I had two small boxes in my pockets.

Each box contained a rock, one was expensive and the other not so much by design. We reached The Rock, and I helped Lydia up on it. She sat on a rock on top of The Rock. I sat on The Rock so I was slightly looking up to her.

I wasn't sure how to begin. I started by telling her how much I loved her. I moved around to get on one knee. She wanted to know what I was doing. So did I.

I said, "Lydia, I have a question for you. I am not sure this is the right time for it, but I decided to ask the question before our trip. I want to know if you will marry me."

She seemed genuinely startled. Her face flushed a little. Her eyes searched my eyes. I held her hand.

She squeezed my hand and asked, "Do you know what you are asking?"

"Yes, I do. What do you think?"

She hesitated and then said, "Yes, I will marry you."

I said, "In that case, I have something for you. I drew out the box with the expensive rocks in it and opened it. Shining against the black velvet was a ring with a marquise cut diamond with four emeralds in the corners. The contrast of the green with the sparkling diamond made it pop.

"This is my gift to you. You may wear it as a symbol of our engagement."

Lydia's eyes teared up. She said, "It is so beautiful. These are the stones we looked at in Charleston."

"Yes, that was my trick to get some idea of what kind of ring you would like."

"Well, that explains that weird visit to the jewelers. For your information I never actually bought your story, but I never imagined it was going to lead to this. You must have spent a fortune on it. I am not sure I can wear it."

"Yes, well, I remembered your feelings on this point. I think you should wear it on special occasions or any time you want, but if there are times you don't want to wear it, I have another ring."

I pulled out the second box and opened it.

She said, "This looks the same."

"But it isn't. It is cubic zirconia, not exactly cheap,

but a lot less expensive. So you can wear the less expensive one on casual occasions and the other one on formal occasions."

With that I was engaged to be married for the second time. It was a strange feeling, a happy feeling.

We walked back to The Cabin. Lydia took off the expensive ring and put on the cubic zirconia one. I put the other one in my safe. I had a safe in my bedroom bolted to the floor. I kept a few valuables in there and my Ruger LCs 9 mm handgun with two full magazines of self defense rounds. I did that because I was security officer in The Cabin, and I didn't want to have to go to the basement gun safe to be armed. Although to be honest, I wasn't sure if I would ever need to be armed. Still, it was a request from Bob.

Paul had instructions on how to open my safe in case I did not return from our trip. He had instructions on my bank lock box and a key for it.

Lydia and I were ready. We needed to head for the airport. We were going to fly to heaven only knows what. It would be an adventure of a lifetime. It might be our last adventure in our lifetime. If things went wrong in the next few days, our lives could change immensely. We were putting it on the line for Danny's memory. The dice had been rolled. We now would just follow the dice around the table.

43

New Jersey

I drove to the airport with Lydia beside me. I was feeling a little calmer since we were in motion. It was hard to tell how Lydia felt. She didn't say much.

We met the pilots. Our lives would be in their hands during the flight and after. They would know a lot about our movements. However, they were secure. Bob made sure of that. He knew them in the military, and when his company was big enough to afford a plane, he hired them. Bob's life seemed to be full of ex-military guys. I am a veteran of the army, but I didn't serve in special ops like the others. I was a desk monkey.

We boarded the plane. The plane was checked out, and we were ready to roll. In minutes we were in the skies over West Virginia and made a swing to the east.

As soon as the plane leveled out on its flight path, the copilot came back and poured coffee for us and served it with coffee rolls from Mama's Restaurant. I like her rolls. She makes them with good ingredients and minimum sugar. She puts cinnamon and raisins on sheets of dough and rolled them up before baking. She didn't drizzle sugar on top like most people do. She knows I don't like it.

We ate generous proportions because it might be a while before we ate again. At least that is what I told myself. The ugly truth is that I like the coffee rolls a lot. I like cinnamon even if it is ground up tree bark.

I looked over at Lydia. She held up her hand, showing me her ring and smiled. I smiled back. I was happy that I had gotten the rings and proposed before the trip. I had debated it with myself for some time. There were arguments for and against. I opted for doing it before the trip because it was not certain what would happen after our mission. We didn't expect any violence other than the bomb. In fact, I had made sure that Lydia didn't sneak her handgun on the trip. There was no need for a gun, and I didn't want the extra risk.

We were leaned back in comfortable seats. I liked flying in the company plane. Once you flew in it, you didn't want to fly commercial, not even first class. This flying was the cat's meow.

That reminded me of The Cat. I asked Jane to feed him while we were gone, but she refused. It seems that The Cat had attacked her over some infraction of a cat rule. Liz begged off for the same reason. They were living in The Cabin, so I thought it would be convenient. Finally, I got Paul to take care of The Cat. Paul promised to feed him and give him fresh water twice a day. I wished there was a way of communicating with The Cat so I could tell him that it might be better if he didn't attack the people who might be feeding him. He probably wouldn't listen though.

I had the greatest urge to go over the plans and think about all the things that could go wrong. Both Mike and Paul had cautioned me against this human reflex. They emphasized that we had done everything possible, everything was set, lean back and follow the plan, don't try to rework the plan, easy to say but hard to do. I reached over and squeezed Lydia's hand.

One thing we had not counted on was having an amateur on the team. We had no data to say that Lydia could hold up under the intense strain. What if she broke down? If she lost her nerve, we would have to abort the mission. Thinking about it made me sweat. I had made an emergency route back to the warehouse in case she lost her nerve before I turned the truck into the driveway. I went over it with Lydia, claiming it was in case of equipment failure.

I felt the plane start to descend, and the pilot came on the intercom to tell us to put away coffee cups and fasten our seat belts. We were going to land in ten to fifteen minutes. I felt a rush.

Snake was there with the chase vehicle to take us to the warehouse. He seemed in a somber mood, which worried me. On the way to the warehouse he let me know that loading the barrels with the ANFO was going to be a lot more work than he anticipated. I reassured him that I would help as soon as I got the truck control system put back in the truck and checked out. He told me that his assistant was taking the steering wheel off while Snake was picking us up so it was ready for me to install the control equipment when we got there.

We pulled into the warehouse parking lot and a door opened. Snake had phoned his helper that we were approaching. We backed in, and the door closed. The truck was there with a pile of ANFO next to it. I could see that hardly any of the ANFO had been loaded into the barrels on the truck.

Lydia sat down to study the route one more time. I started installing the control equipment in the truck. It went smoothly, and soon I was ready to check out the system to make sure something didn't get broken on the trip. We fired up the truck, and I ran through all the control operations. There was one minor glitch, which was easily fixed, and the system was ready to go.

I was sweaty from wearing the hazmat suit, so I was glad that I had remembered to bring a clean, dry set of clothes to wear back on the plane.

I decided to carry the bags of ANFO to the truck. I had Snake load my arms up. I carried several bags at a time and put them in the truck where Snake's assistant could grab them and put them in the barrels. This worked well except the assistant wasn't able to keep up.

Soon we had all the bags in the truck. I got in the truck and helped loading bags into the barrels. It went fast and Snake started to relax.

After the ANFO was in the barrels, I had Snake help me jack the barrel platform in place and block it. We took the jacks off the truck. No sense in blowing them up. I made sure the safety switch on the controller was in the safe position and then loaded and wired the dynamite. The truck was now armed and ready to go.

I was greatly relieved to take off the hazmat suit and cool off. I checked with Snake to make sure our signals were set. It was time to go.

Lydia got in the chase vehicle driver seat. I settled in the back in my simulated truck cab. She started the motor, and I turned the power on the control system. Snake started the truck motor. I verified I could rev the truck engine, and I could move the front wheels from side to side. I jammed the brakes on and signaled Snake to put the truck in gear. We were ready to roll.

Snake's assistant opened the warehouse doors. With a great amount of anxiety, I moved the truck out into the parking lot. Lydia followed it with the chase van. We were on our way.

44

The Big Bang

I had the truck rolling down the road. Lydia was following it. Just like the man who fell off a twenty story building, as he passed the tenth floor someone heard him say, "So far so good."

I was thankful for all the hours of practice, especially the practice of watching the monitors and not the truck. I checked with her verbally once in a while, and she said she was doing fine.

The traffic was light. After what seemed like one hundred miles I could see on the monitors that we were driving down the road that went past the target house. Then Lydia gave me a heads up. We would be at the house in about a minute. I could hear the tension in her voice.

I saw the driveway coming up and got ready. I slowed the truck to make the turn. This was one of the trickiest parts of the trip. My nerves were on edge.

I slowed the truck some more and put on the turn

signal. Suddenly, I had a great urge to laugh and would have done so except I didn't want to startle Lydia. Laughing was not part of the plan. It struck me as funny that I was actually signaling that the truck was turning. Nothing else on this mission was legal so why use the turn signals?

The moment passed quickly as I checked the mirror and swung the truck left in preparation for making a right turn. Lydia had also checked for traffic and said it was okay to swing wide. I turned the front wheels right and the truck started for the driveway. It looked just like the drive I had been practicing on. The truck turned up the driveway. I hadn't dropped a wheel in the ditch. I may have let out a big sigh but I doubt it because I was tense.

The truck continued up the driveway, heading straight for the house. I accelerated the truck to give it some momentum. I could see motorcycles parked in front of the house. As the truck neared the house I could see that there were four motorcycles instead of the planned three. Well, four bikers were going to Hell tonight instead of three. I drove the truck straight for the house and hit the bikes. It was time to detonate.

I tried to get the safety cover over the safety switch up. My hands were so sweaty I couldn't get a grip on the cover. The chase car was going past the house. Lydia asked me if something was wrong. I continued trying to get the cover up, but my hands kept slipping, making me sweat even more. Lydia wanted to know if she should stop because we were getting away from the house. I told her to keep driving slowly.

My hands were just too big and too wet. I finally got a grip on the cover, and it popped up. I turned the safety switch to the fire position. I then had to get the detonation safety cover up, but it was easy. The spring on it wasn't so strong. I put my finger on the button and pushed.

Out of the corner of my eye I saw a slight flash and the monitor screens went dead. Almost immediately we heard an explosion. If we had been close enough, the next thing would have been debris hitting the chase vehicle. I looked back, but we were far enough away so

I couldn't see much.

Lydia sped the chase vehicle up as planned. She wasn't going fast, just a little above the speed limit like most people would be driving. We still had to get on the plane, but I felt a great relief that we had pulled it off.

We drove back to the warehouse, and I removed the equipment from the chase vehicle. Snake and his assistant reinstalled the front seat and switched the license plates back. We dismantled the box I was sitting in and threw the pieces of plywood away. They were meaningless pieces of wood. I put all of the electronics and other parts in boxes that I would take back with me on the plane. We were done. Snake would destroy the stolen license plate and drive the vehicle back to West Virginia after taking us to the plane. Before leaving the warehouse I changed my clothes. Dry clothes felt good.

We got to the plane without trouble. I threw the boxes in the luggage compartment, and we boarded the plane. I made sure Snake had enough money to get to West Virginia. We would pay him his full fee later.

The flight back was like the one east except for two

big differences: one, I was more relaxed and two, we were headed west.

After we got in the air, the copilot served snacks. Sometimes I wished he didn't serve us on the plane. I could get the food myself although it is hard for me to move about. The inside of the plane is about four feet eleven inches, so I practically have to crawl around.

When we were alone, Lydia got close to me and asked me what I was doing as we were passing the house. I told her about the switch cover. It was one thing we hadn't tested in real conditions with sweaty hands. Now that it was over we laughed. They were nervous laughs letting out tension.

Before we left Snake, he gave me the phone he had used to take a video of the explosion. We looked at it in awe. The truck, house, motorcycles, and people had simply disappeared. Perhaps we had used too much ANFO. We were amateurs, but we got the job done.

Snake also confirmed that he saw four guys at the house. There were three on the porch as the truck approached, and then a fourth had come out just before the big bang. I figured it was another biker, and if he was in that house, he was up to no good.

I looked over at Lydia. She caught my look and smiled. We leaned back and rested while we flew home.

45

The Sheriff on the Job

The sheriff was in a mixed mood. On the one hand he was extremely happy, and on the other hand he was a little anxious about the job he had to do that afternoon.

He was happy because a few days ago he was able to go back to one of his smaller gun belts. It was one that he had thrown in the closet when his belly got so big he had to buy a new gun belt, which cost a small fortune, actually, not such a small one. Those belts are expensive.

He had lost fifty pounds. His new life style was working wonders. They didn't call it a diet because a diet implies something temporary. He was on this for the rest of his life, so they called it a new life style.

He had cut out all sodas and most of his beer, and he had eliminated all snack food. To help his complaining body he carried around bags of carrots and sometimes celery. They didn't add any to his weight, and they were crunchy and satisfying to eat. Then to top things off, he and his wife had learned a whole new menu. The combination was working great. His wife was also losing weight, and the weight seemed to be melting off him. He had plateaus, but on average was losing a lot of weight. His doctor didn't want him to lose weight so fast, but this is what happened with his new life style. It was happening naturally. He was not starving although to be honest it seemed like it at times. That was when he pulled out his carrots. Some days he had to go back for more carrots.

The damper on his happiness was a visit he was going to make this afternoon. The sheriff was sure he knew who shot Bob McAvoy right from the beginning. The only problem was that he had no proof of any kind, just a gut feeling and logic, but the logic was based on circumstantial data. The guy in his sights was Delaney Johnson. Everybody called him Del.

The sheriff knew Del had an AR-15, which is a .223 caliber rifle, the same caliber of bullet that the doctors dug out of McAvoy. Of course many people had .223 rifles so that by itself proved nothing. The DA's office would laugh at him if he tried to bring in a case like that. The sheriff checked Del's whereabouts when McAvoy was shot. Del could not account for his time that day. Del had no alibi. Again, this didn't make him guilty.

But Del had a temper. His temper often simmered and then exploded. The calming influence was his wife, Audrey. Audrey kept a lid on Del. Sadly, about six months ago she died of ovarian cancer. That left Del with no calming influence.

The sheriff knew that Del blamed McAvoy for killing his son who had raped Lydia Harding. The sheriff wasn't sure if McAvoy was responsible for the Johnson's kid disappearance or not.

The only fact of the matter was that the kid disappeared when McAvoy and two of his army friends came home for a few days. The sheriff didn't believe in coincidences. Also, McAvoy always was Harding's protector, so logic could say McAvoy killed the boy or made him run away. The only other "fact" was that several people saw the boy drive his car south. The boy was never heard from again. That lent weight to Del's argument. The bottom line though was that there was no proof.

Del was quite vocal about it to the sheriff, but Audrey made him shut up. The sheriff knew that Del might have shut up, but he didn't change his mind. Now that Audrey was gone, Del could do what he wanted. The sheriff figured Del wanted to kill McAvoy.

The sheriff initiated a plan. He visited Del every few days and interviewed him. On each visit he dropped more hints on the case he was building against Del. Del was getting the message, and one day he exploded. He told the sheriff to not come to his house again or there would be trouble. The sheriff thought that trouble to Del meant he might do some shooting. A sheriff cannot afford to be intimidated by such talk, and the sheriff planned another trip this afternoon.

The sheriff finished his lunch and got ready. He went to the locker and got out a bulletproof vest. It was part of the SWAT tactical gear and was a level III vest. He knew if Del used armor piercing bullets, the vest wouldn't stop them. The sheriff was counting on Del using ordinary hunting rounds. He hadn't been able to wear a vest in a long time because of his big belly. He tried the vest on, and to his surprise he was able to fasten it. He thought he might as well wear it. It wasn't going to cost extra, and he thought Johnson was getting close to the edge.

As he left the office, several of the office staff gave him a curious look when they saw him wearing the vest. No one said anything.

He had to move his car seat back because of the vest. It was a tight fit, but he got in the car. He drove slowly out to Del's house. He knew Del would be home this afternoon.

He pulled into the driveway and drove up near the house. He got out and started walking to the house. Before he could get far he felt like he had been hit in the chest with a sledge hammer. There might have been an explosion, but he wasn't sure because he couldn't breathe. Breathing is important, and he was concentrating on it. He was flat on his back. Slowly, he realized he had been shot.

He was worried about being shot again. He couldn't move his left arm at all, but he could move his right arm. He could draw his weapon, but he couldn't use it lying on his back. He slowly and painfully moved his right hand over to his mic and called in an officer-down code. He identified himself and his location. With the task over he felt like passing out. Maybe he was dying, but he didn't think so. He was beginning to feel better, but the pain was bad.

He heard sirens and in minutes Del's yard was filled with cop cars. One officer drove his car up to shield the sheriff, and he got the sheriff in the car. The officer backed his car away from the house to an ambulance.

As they were loading him into the ambulance, he heard a furious barrage of gunfire. He couldn't tell what was happening. Plus, he was in pain.

They took him to the hospital and wheeled him inside. They removed his vest, which hurt like the dickens. An examination proved that the bullet had been mostly stopped by his vest. There was no significant penetration in his body. However, the bullet had struck right over his heart and possibly broke some bones in his chest. He had been close to the rifle when he was shot. The sheriff realized that his weight reduction had saved his life. Without losing weight he would have gone out on the job without his vest.

They checked out his heart. Everything seemed okay, and they decided to release him, but didn't want him to drive for a few days. That was okay because he hurt too much to drive. His wife picked him up at the hospital and took him home.

Later that night a sergeant came to his house to give him a briefing. The sergeant had been in charge as soon as the sheriff was off the scene. The sergeant recounted the shootout. Johnson may have been suicidal. He came out on the porch with his rifle shooting and the deputies shot him dead.

The sheriff was sorry to hear that Delaney was dead. Now, they would never get his story or confession. The sheriff had the sergeant send one of Del's bullets to the state lab to match against the bullet that came out of McAvoy. The sheriff was betting his career that there would be a match. If not, the sheriff would have some tough questions to answer.

46

Back at The Cabin

The plane made a successful landing in West Virginia. I am always relieved when back on the ground. Flying is safer than auto travel, but the fact is landings and takeoffs are the dangerous part of flying.

I got the boxes of parts out of the luggage compartment, and put them in the trunk of the Lexus while Lydia grabbed my change of clothes. I drove to The Cabin. It was too late to check on Mike. I would see him in the morning and give him an update.

It was a good feeling pulling into The Cabin driveway. We were home. I left the boxes of parts in the trunk. I would get rid of them later. I took my bag of clothes, and we went inside. I invited Lydia in for a drink.

We had just gotten in my apartment when Frankie came in. She was obviously upset. She said Mike was okay, but Bob was back in the hospital. He had found out that Lydia went on the mission. He learned that

Mike was in the hospital and started asking questions, which led to the disclosure. He was so upset he jumped out of bed and apparently tore something. He was in some pain, and they were watching him in the hospital for the night. They couldn't find anything wrong with him.

I asked her if Bob was mad at me for taking Lydia. She looked at me as if I had asked if a circle was round. It is. One thing in my favor was that the trip was a success. It is hard to argue with success. I decided that we should have brandies and worry about Bob later. I asked if Mike was well enough for a brandy or at least a briefing. Frankie said he was still in the hospital. He should be released the next day.

In spite of the word on Bob, I felt good. I relaxed and that helped Frankie and Lydia relax. After a brandy, Frankie went back to her apartment.

Lydia hung around, showing no inclination of going to her apartment. I could see that she had something on her mind. It wasn't politic to ask. One had to wait until it came out naturally.

Finally, she said, "I want to stay with you tonight."

I said, "Sure, fine, you can sleep on the couch."

"No, I want to sleep with you."

It was well that there were no feathers around. Otherwise one might have knocked me over.

She continued, "I am not ready for sex, but I would like to sleep with you."

This put a burden on me. It has been my experience that sex for most women is more optional than it is for most men. Women first need to be agreeable and then they need romancing, wine, music and affection to get in the mood and this takes time, time for them to have second thoughts. Men might see an ad in a magazine putting them in the mood. Sleeping with Lydia without sex was going to try my will power to the max.

In addition to that, I was puzzled as to what this meant. Was it just for the night, or was there more to it? I thought it better not to ask at the moment.

Lydia went to her apartment, grabbed a bag and came back in about two minutes. There was an interesting piece of data. She apparently had packed her bag before the trip, so she had been planning this for a while. I was puzzled. Do squirrels and other animals have this much trouble?

We took showers and got in bed. I had gotten used to sleeping alone, but I had a king sized bed, so there was plenty of room except for one thing. The Cat didn't like it when I moved him to make room for Lydia. The Cat went back to his original place. His sleeping pad lay unoccupied. That wasn't going to work, so I moved his pad back where he wanted it. I moved over closer to Lydia.

Lydia liked that better anyway. She wanted to hug up close to me. It was fine with me.

47

The Phone Call

I went back to my routine on Thursday to keep up appearances, plus I had a lot of work to catch up on. I was in my office when my phone rang. It was Vito Bagotti. He was screaming.

I couldn't understand a word he was saying. The only way that I knew who it was by the name on my phone screen. I finally got him calmed down enough so I could get the gist of his message. One thing came through loud and clear.

"You bastards killed my brother-in-law!"

"Excuse me, are you sure you called the right number?"

"Yes, I'm sure. You guys blew up my wife's brother. She is going to blame me. What am I going to do?"

"I don't know what you are talking about."

"You guys blew up that biker's house. My brother-in-law was there visiting. Christ, they can't even find enough for a funeral."

"I am sorry to hear of your brother-in-law's death, but I am not sure why you think I am connected to it."

This line of conversation, if you would call it a conversation, was making me nervous. I wasn't sure how much Bagotti knew and how much was conjecture.

"I heard you guys were tough, but I had no idea you were capable of this kind of violence. I can understand why you went after the bikers because they killed your man. There never was supposed to be any killing or any kind of violence. I told my brother-in-law to make sure this didn't get out of hand."

"What wouldn't get out of hand? What was your brother-in-law up to?"

"He was the connection between me and the bikers. I wanted to fix it so you guys would get behind schedule. If successful, your competitor was going to pay me a lot of money. Nothing like this was supposed to happen. He shouldn't been hanging around with those bikers and involved in killing your guy. God, what am I going to tell my wife?"

"I have no idea what you are going to tell your wife.

I don't know why you called me."

"I called you to tell you this is the end of it. I am not in your league. I want us to go our separate ways."

"Mr. Bagotti, I find all of this mysterious and confusing. However, if you feel we should go our separate ways, then we should do that. Now, you were arranging a large amount of business with your associates. What happens with that? Are you going to recommend against us?"

"Hell no. I'm not crazy. I don't want you bombing my house. I will not stand in your way believe me. I will put you in touch with the right people, and you can deal with them directly. I want no part of it. I will tell them only that you guys are tough, and they should be careful."

With that he hung up the phone. I sat back and thought things over. It was both a surprise and not a surprise to find Bagotti was behind the sabotage. It made perfect sense for him to be behind it, but I really didn't think he had the gall to do such a thing. At least now we knew that the sabotaging was over and our business prospects looked good. This would cheer up Bob. I needed some good news to tell him because he was still little peeved over me taking Lydia on the job in New Jersey. He was beginning to come around because the logic was there, but he still didn't like having her put at such risk. I told him that it was her choice, but he looked at me like I had just told him up was down. With the business back on track, maybe he would soften more.

Before I could leave to go home, my phone rang again. This time it was the sheriff. He wanted to talk with Bob, Mike, Paul and me. Bob and Mike were out of the hospital, but traveling to the sheriff's office would be a hardship on both of them. I suggested he meet us at The Cabin if he didn't mind coming over in the evening. Since Bob funds a large part of the sheriff's campaign, it was no problem for the sheriff to drop by. He would see us around 8 P.M.

I wondered what the sheriff had to say. It made me a little nervous.

48
Bob

Bob was feeling better. He was doing his physical therapy exercises exactly as prescribed. Most people don't. They give up before the benefits slowly kick in. The problem with healing when you get older is that it takes a lot of time and therefore patience and hard work are required. He was a master at that. The doctor's were surprised and pleased at his progress.

He had other things to be happy about, too. He had taken a big chance on Jack and spent a lot of time and money training him. It paid off big time. Just the thing that Bob had always worried about happened. Luckily, he wasn't killed, but he would be out of action for a long time, and that was almost as bad for the business. Jack had taken over the business just like Bob planned. Jack was doing a wonderful job.

There was only one possible shortcoming. Bob didn't think Jack had the experience to plan a strategy for the business for the future. He was fully capable of learning, and Bob made a note to start training Jack as soon as Bob was back on his feet. This was not a surprise. There just wasn't time to get all of the training done.

Another thing that pleased Bob to no end was the developing relationship between Lydia and Jack. Lydia was like a new person. Jack had had a big influence on her. It wasn't clear to Bob how Jack did it, or if he did it on purpose, but Lydia had blossomed in the past year and a half. And finally, Lydia dropped the nonsense about not dating. She was dating Jack.

Frankie was the first to spot it. Frankie told him that Lydia and Jack were falling in love. Bob agreed with the assessment. It did Bob's heart good to see it. Lydia had had such a rough time after her high school tragedy. She deserved some happiness, and it looked like Jack was going to give her happiness.

Nobody had been talking about it much, but it was known that Lydia was sleeping in Jack's apartment. They weren't married or even engaged, but Bob didn't mind as long as they were happy. He trusted Jack to do right by Lydia. Jack was an old school guy and honor and trust were high on his list.

In fact, Bob had almost lost Jack because of a perceived lack of trust on Bob's part. That had scared Bob. He couldn't afford to lose Jack. He vowed to fix that blunder.

Lastly, the business was back on track. The sabotaging was over. Jack had led the guys in a team effort to kill the guys who killed Danny, and at the same time stopped the sabotaging permanently. Bob was still sore over Jack taking Lydia on the job, but he could see the logic. It was Frankie who really brought him around, pointing out that Lydia needed to be her own person and make her own decisions. Going on the job was her decision, not Jack's. Once Bob saw that, he cooled off and also decided he needed to think about Lydia differently. She wasn't a kid any more, and she was better mentally. She didn't need his protection. She had Jack, and she was her own person.

He knew Jack was planning a celebration dinner. That would be a lot of fun. Bob had been practicing walking. He wanted to walk to the dinner and be able to stand up and toast Jack.

Tonight the sheriff was coming to meet with him, Jack, Paul and Mike. He didn't know what that was about, but he had heard rumors about the sheriff. The sheriff was almost killed by Del Johnson. Then the sheriff's deputies shot and killed Johnson. Bob had a growing suspicion that he knew what had happened, and how wrong he had been. Maybe that was what the meeting was about and Bob would find out for sure.

49

The Sheriff's Visit

The sheriff got into his official car. This was a business trip to The Cabin. It was also a pleasure trip. He was going to tell them what he had found out. He was going to have trouble not gloating. Well, darn it, maybe he would gloat a little. He deserved it. How often do you get to gloat? And this was a duesy.

He had gone out on a limb on the McAvoy shooting. McAvoy and his merry band of men thought the sheriff couldn't solve the case. Well, if it had been an out of town hit as McAvoy believed, then the sheriff wouldn't have solved it, but that wasn't the case.

He had taken risks talking with Johnson. Just thinking about it made his chest hurt. How is it that in the movies and on TV people get shot in a vest and laugh it off? In real life it hurts like hell. He had been shot in a vulnerable spot in his chest, and it had almost killed him even with his vest. A shock big enough like that directly on your heart can stop your heart.

As soon as all of this was over, he was going to celebrate being alive. He was feeling good with his new life style. He was still losing weight, and he wasn't so hungry now. His wife was losing weight, too. It was changing their lives. They were able to get out and do things much easier, and they had more energy. They were going to have to buy new clothes.

Most of all though, he wanted to celebrate surviving being shot in the chest. Modern technology was great. In the old days, he would have been dead. Also, if he hadn't lost a lot of weight, he would be dead. His chest was still sore, but it was getting better. A sore chest is much better than a chest with a hole in it. His chest had a small cut, but it was more like a dent than a hole.

The whole thing lit a fire under his wife. She was in favor of their new life style, but after seeing how it saved his life, she had become a fanatic. Now, he was losing even more weight. He was already down sixty pounds. He hoped that he didn't disappear.

He pulled off the main highway and started up the driveway to The Cabin. It was a nice drive through the beautiful old hardwood trees. He loved coming here to shoot. He didn't get in The Cabin often, but when he did, he was awed by the splendor. It pays to have money.

McAvoy had made a pile of money, and he wasn't afraid of spreading it around. The sheriff benefited from McAvoy's largesse. The sheriff didn't feel bad about taking McAvoy's money for campaigning. It helped him win elections, and Bob had never made an unreasonable demand in return.

Bob spent money in style, and The Cabin was a great example. It was a beautiful building. The sheriff had heard about the parties there, but he had never been to one. The people who had been there often spoke about the huge rooms and the eye popping amenities. Momma told him about the fancy kitchen they had there. The sheriff was looking forward to going inside.

He parked his car in the lot by The Cabin. He knew he was on camera since he had turned off the highway. It didn't bother the sheriff.

It was an official visit, so he was wearing his

uniform. He was so accustomed to wearing his gun, he didn't give it much thought. It was part of his being he had worn it so many years. Still he was conscious of the fact he was wearing it in a private home.

He rang the door bell, and the door was immediately opened, confirming his suspicion that he was on camera. Paul Jackson opened the door, and he escorted the sheriff to Bob's apartment.

They went in, and there was McAvoy, Randall, and Clayton waiting for them. There was no need for introductions. The sheriff knew them all.

The sheriff started by asking Bob how he was doing. They had grown up together, and the sheriff had a genuine interest in Bob's health. Bob had taken a nasty shot to the chest, and he didn't have a vest on like the sheriff did.

He was pleased to find that Bob was doing well. His body was healing, and his spirits were high. Bob would feel even better after the sheriff delivered his message. He thought it best if he charged into it.

"I asked to meet with you men so you can hear it

directly from me before the media gets hold of it. I have determined who shot Bob."

The room was quiet. God forgive him, but the sheriff was loving the moment. He continued.

"I suspected Del Johnson of the deed. I was leaning on him, which is why he lost his cool and shot me. That gave me the opportunity to test bullets fired from his gun and see if they matched the bullet taken out of Bob's chest. I just got the lab results back today. There was a match. That proves the gun used to shoot Bob was Johnson's gun. Furthermore, Johnson had no alibi for his whereabouts on the day Bob was shot. He had motive, means, opportunity, and owned the weapon used. In a court of law he would have been convicted with this evidence. Sadly, as you know, he died in a gun battle with my department."

Bob was the first to speak, "I assume that you are referring to the fact that Johnson thought I had something to do with his son's disappearance. Why did he wait this long? Why now?"

"Because his wife died about six months ago from

cancer. She was keeping a lid on him. Once she was gone, he had nothing left to live for, and he felt it was time to even the score. This is speculation on my part. The only fact is that his wife died six months ago."

"Well sheriff, I think Johnson must have been crazy shooting me. I am grateful that you found the culprit. That means we can get rid of all these guards and our lives can get back to normal. I can use some normal. This has been a rough time. We all congratulate you on your success."

Jack spoke up, "Sheriff I am organizing a dinner party this Saturday to celebrate our good fortunes. We are happy that Bob is healing so well, and our business has just enjoyed a breakthrough. Now that you have solved this mystery, we have one more thing to celebrate. I invite you and your wife to our party. We can celebrate your success."

"That sounds great. I would be pleased to attend along with my wife. I can also celebrate being alive. Johnson came very close to turning my lights out."

The sheriff was relieved to find out the dress was

casual. He had no idea what they wore here. They might have been showing up in tuxedos for all he knew.

The sheriff left The Cabin a happy man. He could see how much the group was relieved, knowing for sure who shot Bob and that there was no longer a threat. He was also very pleased to have been invited to their dinner party. His wife would enjoy it, too. They might even have to get off the new life style wagon just for this celebration.

50

The Dinner

I was beside myself with excitement. I was looking forward to the dinner in the evening. I hadn't been this happy in years. For one thing the reports from New Jersey indicated that the police were convinced that the bombing was done by a rival biker gang. That was excellent. The longer they believed that and the longer they failed to investigate, the more evidence would be lost.

I was also happy to hear Mike's report on Bagotti's brother-in-law. He wasn't an innocent bystander. He was a member of the biker gang and one of the top guys, which explained why he was at the house that night. He was more involved in Danny's killing than Bagotti knew.

Mike had come to me last night in private. He felt bad about not being able to go to New Jersey. I told him if you're sick you're sick. He shook my hand and thanked me profusely. It was a nice gesture, but his thanks was not really necessary. In our group friends help friends.

Later, I found out he thanked Lydia for subbing for him and gave her a hug. I wish I had been there to see it. I know she is a little afraid of Mike. I rather think it made her feel good though. She was proud of having played an important role in a Club activity.

Lydia and I had been working all morning getting the dinner ready. Momma and her daughter were coming over in the evening to do the final cooking and serving, but we were doing the preparation, and some of the food would take all day to simmer. Simmering is one of the secrets of good cooking. Americans have pretty much lost that art. Everyone is in a rush today. They want fast food. Well, really good food isn't fast.

We were going to have spaghetti with meat balls and veal Parmesan. What was going to take the time was simmering the spaghetti sauce in a big pot on the stove. We were using tomatoes from Marty and my organic farming operation. Lydia and I had peeled them and ran them through a sieve to remove the seeds. That also breaks the fibers, making the sauce smooth. We used tomato sauce and tomato paste that Louise and I had made.

The sauce would simmer for most of the day with my periodically stirring it with a wooden spoon. We made the meat balls from organic meat grown on a local farm and put them in the refrigerator ready to be cooked later.

All of this was a lot more fun with Lydia working by my side. We worked together to set the table, and she helped prepare the ingredients for cooking. The real fun part was when we touched each other. She was excited about the announcement we were going to make after the dinner. I hadn't seen her this happy before. It was a joy hearing her laugh and giggle.

From time to time some of the gang wandered down to the kitchen, but I shooed them away. This was a moment for Lydia and me. I think the gang caught on because they stayed away.

The Cat was a different story. He lumbered in the kitchen. He could smell the cooking. Tough cookies. He had his own food. The only problem was that if ignored, he might get mad and attack one of us. I took him up to my apartment, gave him fresh water, stirred his food with my finger and gave him a pet. He felt loved, ate and went back to sleep.

Momma closed up her restaurant and made it to The Cabin as soon as she could. I met her in the kitchen, and we went over the plans. I liked working with her. She is an excellent cook. She cooks good old fashion country food, but I had taught her some gourmet dishes. She learned fast because she knew the basics.

As soon as she was set, I headed for my apartment to get ready. Lydia was in her apartment getting ready. I was finishing my dressing when she came over. She took my breath away. She had a little makeup on, and she was simply ravishing.

I could see she was hiding something. She came out with a flower for my lapel. She knew I loved flowers. It was a thoughtful touch. I went to the refrigerator and got out her corsage and pinned it on her dress. I didn't get flowers for the other women. This was a special night for Lydia and me. Lydia and I were dressing up a little and the others would be in casual clothes.

We went downstairs to meet the guests. People were gathering in the large bar area. I was surprised to see Bob standing at the bar. A close look revealed the fact that he was using the bar as a crutch. Still, he was on his feet and looking happy.

Luckily, Momma announced that dinner was ready before everyone got tight on the pre-dinner drinks.

Momma's daughter was helping. It was a big group and there was a lot of food to bring out. We were going to have a feast. People had a choice of spaghetti with meat balls or the veal or both. We had a nice tossed salad and other bits of food. The amount of food was scandalous, but it was delicious. We had several bottles of Chianti wine and Lydia and I shared a bottle of white wine. Rebels.

Before we started eating, Bob got up to say thanks for all of our good fortunes. It was an emotional moment. Unspoken was the thanks that we had found Danny's killers and had dealt with them. This had to be unmentioned because the sheriff and his wife were sitting at the table.

We wrapped up dinner with a dessert. For a change I didn't make the dessert. Momma made it. It was a black forest cake with a creamy frosting and maraschino cherries on top. It was a cake to die for. It was enhanced with gourmet coffee.

After dinner I asked people to go into the library where there would be an announcement. Lydia grabbed my arm and hung on. I didn't know if she needed the support or she thought I needed it. Maybe she just wanted to be close to me.

In the library was an easel covered with a cloth. Lydia looked at it and back at me with a puzzled look on her face. Only two of us knew what was under the cloth. I knew and Frankie knew.

I made sure everyone had a drink, and then Lydia and I stood to make our announcement. Lydia had been either hiding her ring or not wearing it so no one other than Frankie had a clue about our engagement. She quietly put the expensive ring in its place on her finger and put her hand on my arm with the ring showing.

I said, "Lydia and I would like to announce our engagement to be married."

Lydia held up her hand showing everyone her ring. People were excited, and I calmed them by saying that there was one more disclosure.

Frankie helped me. We pulled the cloth off the easel disclosing a painting of Lydia and me on The Rock. The painting was done by Frankie. It captured the mood of The Rock exactly. It was a private place known only to Lydia and me, so I was worried that Lydia would be offended by me having Frankie do the painting. It was the only painting that I knew of that she had done by request. It was a gift for Lydia.

I watched Lydia carefully to gage her reaction. I think my heart stopped while I waited. Frankie was more sanguine. She had assured me that Lydia would love it. She and Lydia had become best friends, so I trusted her judgment, but I was still nervous. I was nervous until I saw Lydia's face.

When she saw the painting, tears of happiness made their way down her cheeks, taking parts of her makeup with them. After staring at the painting for a moment, she came to me and kissed me passionately. She had never displayed this much affection in front of others. I kissed her back. She whispered in my ear, "Jackson, you make me so happy."

My real name is Jack. Lydia calls me Jackson in private. It was her term of endearment for me. She said it was softer than Jack.

It then turned into a party. People came up to Lydia and me and congratulated us. We got a lot of hugs. The sheriff and his wife approached. He shook my hand. He had a strong grip, reminding me what a big man he is. He is a big dude.

Bob and Jane came to us. It was an emotional moment. Bob and Jane were like parents to Lydia. I had a momentary fear that I should have asked them permission to marry Lydia.

Bob wanted to know when we were going to get married. We hadn't set a date. Bob and Jane informed us that when we got married we could have their apartment in The Cabin.

Later, Bob came to me in private and said that he had heard that Lydia and I were more or less living together. He suggested that in that case we should move into their apartment right away.

After some dancing, people started leaving. Lydia and I waited until everyone was gone, and we went back to my apartment, which had become our apartment.

We got undressed to get ready for bed. Lydia was not as shy about disrobing in front of me. She put on a beautiful nightie. We got into bed and for the first time we made love.

Acknowledgments

I greatly appreciate the work of my editor, Cynthia Henrich, who in spite of serious health problems, corrected many errors.

I thank beta reader Ron Temple for finding errors and suggesting story improvements.

I thank my wife, Rose Sisson, for artistic assistance on the cover design.

Finally, I thank Ron Temple and Cynthia Henrich for suggesting ways of making the book title more relevant to the story.

As usual, I appreciate all the help, but in the end I am responsible for any remaining errors.

Albert

Made in the USA
San Bernardino, CA
03 April 2016